SHOCK WAVE

SHOCK WAVE

DOROTHY SALISBURY DAVIS

Charles Scribner's Sons   New York

Copyright © 1972 Dorothy Salisbury Davis

This book published simultaneously in the United States of America and in Canada—Copyright under the Berne Convention

All rights reserved. No part of this book may be reproduced in any form without the permission of Charles Scribner's Sons.

A—5.72(V)

PRINTED IN THE UNITED STATES OF AMERICA

Library of Congress Catalog Card Number 77-37200

SBN 684-12748-2 (Trade cloth)

Design by Bob Antler

for Burroughs, editor and friend

ONE

My first big assignment had been in my home state, Illinois, an interview with a man who might some day be President. I went down from Chicago to Springfield on the St. Louis Flyer. That was in 1951, over twenty years ago. The man, of course, is dead without ever having been President, and some who became President are dead. I have covered these deaths. I have written about so much violence. Everybody knows that violence makes news, but now it seems news makes violence. That is today's difference, I think.

In the intervening twenty years I had not had an assignment, I had not free-lanced a story that—how shall I put it?—very simply, made me feel so good. So when Mike Fischer, the editor of *Saturday Magazine*, asked me what I knew of Illinois, I wanted to say several things at once, and wound up saying only that I grew up there.

"Know anything about big Steve Higgins?"

"He's the last of something they're always saying somebody's the last of."

"Baron, boss, or bullshit artist?"

"Probably all of them," I said.

Mike tried to see clear through me. That's the feeling I get when he's about to pin me down to an assignment. "There's a story, don't you think?"

"It's old hat, Mike."

"Not when it's filed by Kate Osborn, it isn't."

I made a gesture of demur, and asked him when he expected me to leave. He looked at his watch. It was a silent gag that ran through our relationship.

We went downstairs and had a drink while Mike told me what had put him onto Steve Higgins, the rumor of a power struggle between him and the mayor of Chicago. A battle of dinosaurs, Mike said, and quickly added, "Nevertheless." We went over the Higgins interests that we knew about: a couple of radio stations, a newspaper chain, coal mining, oil, vending machines, and the downstate farm where he lived most of the time. It was called The Hermitage after Andrew Jackson's home in Tennessee.

I said, "Do you know anything connecting him with the State University at Venice?" There was something at the back of my mind but I couldn't dig it out.

"You'll find it," Mike said. "And then there's the blacks and the whites down there. A powder keg. It would be interesting if that blew up while you were on top of it."

2

"Very."

He suggested that I fly to St. Louis and then drive back to Venice when I said I proposed to headquarter there. But I wanted to start the assignment, going down by train from Chicago, and I told Mike why.

"A sentimental journey," he mocked gently.

"The perfect warm-up," I said. "What's more sentimental than politics?"

"There's more down there than politics, Kate. If there wasn't, I wouldn't make the investment. I think it's another big one for you, gal."

＊　＊　＊

There was a run affectionately called the Night Train leaving Chicago in the late afternoon. It carried a combination diner and club car. The porter, taking charge of my luggage, advised me to get a table early. It was the custom of the regulars to settle in there as soon as the tickets were collected and stay throughout their journey. Dinner was served out of Champagne-Urbana.

I did go into the diner early. It was like walking into a men's club where all the members turn at once to question the presence of a woman. The hostility eased off as soon as I was taken over by the head-waiter, the danger of my intrusion on preserved ground presumably averted. The headwaiter, a cheerful, gold-toothed black man in a white coat that rustled, seated me by the window at a table set for two with an arsenal of silver at each place. He gave me the option of facing forward, which meant going toward the sun, or riding backward. I chose the prairie sunset. It is one of the things I have missed, sometimes achingly. I ordered a Bourbon Presbyterian.

"Oh, yes!" He said it as though it were a concoction for which he had himself nostalgia.

The whole staff was pleasant and courteous, and briefly I forgot the black man's anger, to which I had grown accustomed in my America. The bourbon was Old Taylor. The waiter wrung the neck of the miniature bottle and uncapped the ginger ale and soda. I don't drink bourbon anymore, and I occasionally use ginger ale to baste ham during baking, but my father used to drink the mixture, and the aroma took me back to the farm living room on a Sunday afternoon. In this context it tasted fine.

I found myself picking out the native faces among those before me, men I would have said were returning home downstate. "American Gothic" could have been painted of any generation. Pitchforks may be obsolete and collarless shirts out of fashion, but those stern faces mounted on necks like fence posts are as durable as the plains against the sky. I speculated on their households and occupations and what their wives were like, and on why I was not married to one of them instead of to an archeologist I had met in an Israeli bomb shelter. I did not have the answer, but it was a question I never failed to ask myself in one way or another whenever I passed that way.

The waiter came and asked me if I minded sharing my table. I did, but I said No. The dining car had become crowded. The man he brought was ramrod straight, gray-eyed, and his blond hair was cut to the old convention. I judged him to be in his early or mid-

4

forties, not much older than myself. His thanks were more a sound than a word, and I merely nodded my welcome. Neither of us was committed. He ordered Scotch and soda. I returned to my contemplation of the setting sun: with its spangled rays, a great wheel of chance.

For a time I was aware of him only as a reflection in the windowpane—an intrusion there also—who for his part was staring at his own thoughts, his eyes hard on the saltshaker or some other object on the table. Now and then the trace of a down-turning smile played at the corners of his mouth. He had to work to make that mouth seem strong, I thought. He kept trying to toughen it. I kept trying to see through his reflection to the sunset, but it was no use: a human struggle was going on across the table from me. Or the replay of a struggle: I clearly remember thinking that before we had spoken a word to one another. I took for granted, despite the conservative business suit and the grooming, that he was connected with the university at Venice. Then he too looked out the window, and it was only a matter of a second or two before our eyes met in the glass. I turned my head and met his gaze directly.

"Venice State?" he asked, as though wondering where he might have seen me before.

"No . . ." I tried to make it sound tentative, not terminative. "But you are, aren't you?"

He nodded.

"Science?"

A little arch of the eyebrows: I had hit it straight on and he was pleased. "Randall Forbes, physics department," he said, and raised himself an inch or so from the chair.

"My name is Osborn," I murmured. "What kind of physics?"

"High energy."

"The one with the big bang."

"Or the big bust—in today's perspective."

"I suppose you are out of fashion," I mused. His chin went up. "But then I should not suppose fashion to be of great concern to the scientist."

"I'd go so far as to say fashion is corruptive. Of course, some people would say the same thing of three meals a day."

I laughed. His drink came. He said Cheers, drank, and sighed at the pleasure it gave him. I was trying to place his accent: educated; I caught no trace of regionalism.

"Does the name Daniel Lowenthal mean anything to you, Mrs. Osborn?" His eyes had moved briefly to my wedding band.

"The Nobel Laureate? Oh, yes."

The slightest change in expression, no more than a sniff, the contraction of his nostrils: he had hoped I would have recognized the name Randall Forbes also. "I took my doctorate under Lowenthal . . . in the days of fame and fashion. We were a great team, every man in the group a theorist worth the name. All scattered now—like our science—except for the old man and me. He's chairman of the department at Venice State. Or did you know that?"

I shook my head. "But I might have if I'd thought about it."

"Then you *are* at the university?"

Again I shook my head that I was not.

"I'm reasonably sure you don't sell cosmetics," he

blurted out, his color rising. He tried to amend: "By which I mean, I don't mean . . ." He threw up his hands.

"That I should go and put on some lipstick?" I prompted mockingly.

"Oh, God." Then: "Maybe you do sell cosmetics— to those who need them."

"You're safe," I said, smiling. "I'm a newspaper woman, Professor Forbes."

He refrained from comment, taking no more chances. We both ordered another drink when the waiter brought us menus. "I *did* meet a woman on the train once who sold cosmetics. I was married then, and, do you know, she arrived at the house the next day and told my wife that I suggested she call?"

"She made the sale," I said.

"You're right, where I'd have said she hadn't a chance to make a nickel. I really don't know women at all." He studied the menu and then glanced up at me. "Order something on the dark side and I'll stand us a bottle of wine. Please, don't protest. I have something to celebrate."

"I wouldn't dream of protesting."

This time I omitted the ginger ale from the mix when the drinks came. We both ordered Louisiana oysters and the prime ribs of beef.

I lifted my glass. "To whatever it is that you're celebrating, Professor."

"I wouldn't want this to get in the papers yet."

"It's off the record," I assured him, trying not to be solemn.

Still he hesitated. Two small points of color remained in his cheeks, the rest having drained away. He plunged ahead: "I'm celebrating three hundred thousand dollars, a research grant to the department which no one would have given us a microscopic chance of getting. I went after it."

"And got it?"

He rocked back and forth and smiled as he nodded. He did not smile often or easily and the smile looked forced, but the flush rose again to his cheeks and his eyes were dancing; even his shoulders quivered as he said, "Today."

"Congratulations," I said. I had not known three hundred thousand could be so significant a sum in current research. "What will you do with it?"

"Gain tenure," he said, and then broke into laughter at his own impromptu response. "You see, the truth will out. If anyone else had said that of me, I would have chewed his head off. Why, we'll finish experiment in progress, I think. Whatever the chief decides. My own qualification—if I'm permitted to impose it— nothing useful. Do you know what I mean? Nothing deliberately useful."

"Pure research."

"Exactly. So Goddamned pure . . ." He thought about that for a moment. "I wish I could tell you what it was like when the old boy was my age and I was his student, the propositions we worked out together, the fantastic combinations we'd throw at one another. . . . It was like playing tag among the stars."

"Is it that much different today?"

I wished I had not asked that, for he became quite glum. "Oh, yes. I have a graduate student who refers to his thesis as a pile of shit."

"Nevertheless, he wants his degree," I said.

"Who knows what they want nowadays? The communication lines are down. It's an accident when we reach one another at all."

"Then why do you teach? Your interest is in basic research."

"I must!" he said, an impatient crescendo to his voice. "The two things are inseparable."

"I wasn't baiting you," I said quietly.

"I know . . ." He gave a dry little laugh. "You must understand also: neither government nor industry is competing with the university for my services."

I nodded sympathetically.

He ordered a half-bottle of Chablis to be served with the oysters, and a Médoc '64 to go with the beef. "One wants something without too much bottom since it's been traveling," he explained. "Not that there's a great choice."

"Anywhere," I said, and returned to the subject of physics. "Yet the whole business of fusion remains to be opened up, yes?"

"Yes," he said with a mixture of surprise and tolerance. He had not expected even that of me. I was put in mind of Sam Johnson's woman preacher and the dog who walked on its hind legs.

I said, "I speak out of a kind of controlled ignorance."

"And I out of a limited knowledge. Such humility makes us unique, wouldn't you say?"

"It ought to put us in tune with the young—who think themselves so honest."

"It ought," he said, "but it don't."

Presently I asked, "How do the kids today feel about Lowenthal?"

"How do you mean?"

"Politically. When I was in college he was more famous for his leftish politics than for his science almost."

"I have no idea."

The question rankled, I supposed because he was not himself political. Instinctively I knew that of him. I was sorry to have dampened the little glow which seemed to have ignited between us. I said, "He will be pleased at your success . . . in Chicago."

"Good God, yes." He came to life again before my eyes. "I hope he won't make too much of it. After all, he's been recipient to grants of considerably larger sums than that . . . and from rather more distinguished foundations than the Bernard Reiss." He thought about what he had just said. "That's ungrateful of me, isn't it?"

I finished my highball. The waiter took away the glass before he opened the wine. He ceremonially poured a few drops. Forbes crinkled his nose after tasting the wine.

I said, "What do the foundation people really expect of you, Professor?"

"Ha! How did you know?"

"My husband is often dependent on grants. He's an archeologist."

"Clean heat. You had it right away," Forbes said, about as interested in my husband as I had been in the cosmetics saleswoman. "That's what fusion means to them. They want ecology and energy in the same package. It's quite a trick. And yet, you know, the Russians have come up with a conversion advance, which if it works"—he shrugged—"they're way ahead of us."

I could imagine him using that argument on the foundation, and I thought, the purer the purpose, the more practical the pitch.

"Does it trouble you, as a scientist, that the Soviets are ahead?"

"It troubles me not to know what they know. Yes. But that's all. This nuclear converter of theirs is out of my field, but one wants to know. Nowadays one has to know. It seems like they have bypassed the pollutant-making phase in transforming energy to power . . . I'll explain if you like."

"Please do," I said, and I was sure as he went on, that in informing my ignorance, he was reliving one of his best moments with the foundation representatives.

The oysters came, shimmering and icy cold on their half-shells, and we commenced a dinner that proclaimed us both sensualists, something neither of us would have expected of the other. We talked of music and the movies. We did not expect to meet again, and were therefore more personal than we might otherwise have been. We were enjoying an intimacy all blossom and no roots, I felt, satisfied in the transience of our meeting.

We were having coffee when Forbes looked at his watch. "I must pull myself together," he said. "We're less than a half-hour out of Venice. You know, when I first came down here, I always said, Venice, Illinois, there being but one Venice that could stand on its own in my opinion. Now I say, Venice, Italy, when I mean that other city."

"And I am glad to have met it first through you, Professor. Shall we ask for our checks?"

"You're getting off at Venice also?" he said slowly,

as though picking his way from one word to the next, as though in fact he felt that I had deceived him.

I wanted to assure him that I did not expect anything of him in Venice. I said, "Yes. There isn't any secret about my assignment, Professor. I work for *Saturday Magazine*. We're expecting to do a story on Steve Higgins."

He put on that downward smile again. Then he laughed aloud and said, "Good luck!"

"I didn't think he would be your man," I said, trying to make light of it.

"Nor I his, you may be sure."

"That part I didn't know."

"You'll see. You'll see."

We exchanged amenities after paying our respective bills, and parted with a handshake when I offered my hand and it would have been rude of him to ignore it. But he had quite turned off.

                    *   *   *

The train stopped in Venice a few minutes later. It wasn't nine o'clock, but the railway station was closed. I soon saw that it had been that way for years. Nor was there any sign of a cab. Forbes, leaving from the dining car, was the only other person on the platform. He strode alongside the train as it moved out and helped me haul my luggage to the taxi phone box. The phone had been pulled out by the roots.

"That's a familiar sight, but I didn't expect it here," I said.

"Why? Don't you think we're civilized?"

I was cut by his bitter wit, and when he had gone,

walking home and having promised to have a cab sent for me, I had to fight a feeling of desolation. What I could see of Venice did not help. There was a kind of white silence on the town. The few cars that passed, and the fewer people on the street, seemed like etched figures in a shooting gallery, an impression I better understood on realizing how much light there was. Even the stores, closed for the night, were aglow though not a soul moved within them. And nothing suggested the presence of the university in the town.

I paced. I waited. I could not have sat down if I wanted to. The benches had long since been torn away. Their pale outlines remained in the scarred paint of the building. The tracks sang mournfully of the distancing train. I was reminded of the Great Depression in the thirties. Not that I could remember it well. I have sometimes felt deprived for having been too young to appreciate it. On the Venice railway platform I no longer felt so deprived. Then the cab came.

TWO

Swift and heavy clouds were traveling the sky when I stepped out of the Mardi Gras Inn the next morning. The hotel was fake New Orleans of another century, but it was newly built, what you might call a credit-card hotel, and after the bleakness of my arrival, I had not minded the exaggeratedly hearty welcome. I also appreciated the new white Chevrolet Impala that was waiting in response to my order for a car rental.

Now and then the sun broke out while I drove the twenty miles to The Hermitage. Briefly: the clouds rode herd on one another. The air was clear, wind-pure, and frost-sharp. It was the month of March at its most dramatic. Immediately outside Venice, oil pumps scattered the countryside. A few miles on, the oil fields gave way to farmland, rich, autumn-plowed brown-black earth and stubbled pasture where dairy cattle foraged. There were orchards as uniform in planting as the cornfields of my childhood. When I neared The Hermitage, I could see the beginning of the Shawnee Hills in the distance, and on either side of the road pine trees grew among the shaggy hickory and oak.

A lame attendant opened the iron gates to The Hermitage. He saluted and waved me through. In the rearview mirror I watched him close the gates. I wondered in what war he had been maimed. Or what mine disaster.

The fine gravel whistled beneath the wheels. The driveway curved through a sparse woods where, even in the fullness of summer, there would always be a seepage of sunlight. I caught sight of two people riding horseback parallel to me through the woods. They spurred the horses and I slowed down so that I had only parked the car when Higgins and a woman companion rode up. He dismounted, threw the reins over the horse's head—a beautiful bay with froth at the bit —and gave them to the woman while he came to shake my hand.

"I'm glad to see you've something sensible on your backside," he said, as I stepped from the car. He was tall, handsome still at sixty-eight, with very sharp blue eyes. He introduced the woman simply as Laurie. She was plumpish, a little hard-looking, I'd have said in her late forties: secretary, companion, and the rest. Higgins bade her give me her horse with nary a question as to whether I wanted it or not. So I exchanged my cape for Laurie's sheep-lined jacket and mounted Jezebel in my Bergdorf Goodman pant suit. Jezebel proposed to take the bit away from me at once, and Higgins, I felt, deliberately danced his bay around as he remounted, making the mare more skittery. I put my heels to her ribs and reined toward the bridle path. Again I heeled her and bent low over her withers. I did not let up until she reached a gallop. I let her slow down gradually, but took her on for another fifty yards before turning back.

Higgins' face creased in a grin, but all he said was, "Let's go round the house first."

We rode across the frozen lawn in front of the mansion. It was Southern-Colonial with Corinthian columns and a railed veranda clear across the second story. On either side of the ground floor was a one-room annex with windows overlooking the estate in three directions. For me it had both grace and warmth, and I said so. I asked if the bricks had been manufactured on the grounds; such was the case at Jackson's Hermitage.

"No, but we've used Illinois granite." He reined up alongside a domed, slender-columned shrine imitative of a Greek temple. In this he had again followed Jackson. He removed his hunting cap. "I've had my wife, Nancy, buried here. There's room for me. I never did take up more than my half the bed." He scratched his head and put the cap back on. "Some will tell you I didn't take that up a lot of the times. You'll have to decide for yourself whether or not to believe them."

We rode on to the stables where a groom came out and kept our horses moving while we went inside. Higgins still trained jumpers. He had given up the races, having, after years of trying, come up with a winner at Churchill Downs only to have the horse disqualified. "I felt like I'd flunked out of the social register when I had no business trying for it in the first place. So I said to hell with it."

There were ten horses, one handsomer than the next. Two mares were heavy with foal. Higgins went in the stall and put his arm underneath the neck of one of them, hugging the face to his own. I was reminded of my father who loved animals better than he loved most people.

He showed me the harness room and then a furnished apartment upstairs. "I've been known to stay out here myself—when it's time for the foals to drop."

Outdoors again, we rode through the barnyard and down a lane to a field where a herd of Guernsey cattle grazed on sorghum stubble. Forty head, I estimated.

"Second highest herd in the state for butterfat. I don't want to be first. That's hard on my dairyman, but it's a funny thing: there's a point in many a competition where I don't want to be number one. What do you make of that?"

I thought about it and laughed.

"What does that mean?"

"Well, I was thinking, Mr. Higgins: if that's really so, what am I down here for?"

"You mean *Saturday Magazine* wouldn't be wasting its number one gal on a number two tycoon?"

"Something like that."

"Well, it'll be interesting to see if they know Steve Higgins better than he knows himself. Isn't that a grand herd of cattle?"

"I've never seen one more beautiful, and I grew up with Guernseys."

"I grew up with Holsteins you might say—the human variety," he said. "In East Moline."

It took me a moment to realize that he meant he had grown up in a mixed neighborhood.

We turned into the lane again and headed in the direction of the woods. "That ought to have had some advantages," I said.

"As a matter of fact you're right. I understand those people. And some of them dig me. I've put a half-dozen colored boys through law school, and what my white brethren think of me for that, you can just about imagine. One of my boys went to the state legislature last year. I won't say I'm not prejudiced, Mrs. Osborn, but I'm not bigoted."

I was going to have to mull that one over. "Isn't it a pretty fine distinction, Mr. Higgins?"

"That's the kind of distinctions I like to make. Anybody can make the big ones—men from boys, sheep from goats, and so forth. And call me Steve. Everybody else does."

We passed through a hunt gate, which Higgins left open. I saw the jumps in the field ahead. "A real course," I said.

"If you're willing to stay with us till Easter, I'll organize a hunt in your honor. How would you like that?"

I gave a little laugh, weighing the idea. "I don't really know."

We galloped the length of the field and entered the woods by another hunt gate. I could have sworn I glimpsed a fox.

"There's red fox in here all right," Higgins said. "It's a damn shame, but the law says we got to drag hunt. And the thing that makes no sense, I can shoot

18

any damn fox I see on my property. But I'd be the first to say it: a civilization depends on its hypocrisy."

I had to agree with him at the moment, for I was thinking that the idea of a hunt in my honor was more to my liking for the absence of live prey. But, of course, I would not say so.

I washed in the bathroom off the library and settled in before the fire with my notebook. Higgins had stopped at what he called the staff room to sign letters. Passing through the hall, I had heard telephones ringing and the muffled clack of typewriters. There was a good copy of Sully's portrait of Jackson over the fireplace. I wished I liked Jackson, as I did Jefferson, say. Once I had, passionately, but only once, the year Truman ran against Dewey for the Presidency.

When Higgins joined me, he poured two whiskeys without consultation. "Water if you say so, but it's better bourbon than you've ever tasted, young lady."

"Just ice, please."

He disapproved of ice also, but tonged a piece into the glass. Someone had set out the whiskey, water, and ice, and had lit the fire, anticipating our return. He brought the drinks and, after the merest dart of his eyes to my notebook, said, "I like my men he and my women she and my whiskey straight. Cheers."

He lifted his glass.

"You and your fine distinctions," I said.

He gave a bark of laughter.

The whiskey was deep amber, soft, and aromatic.

"It's the Ozark water, hickory kegs, and love— though I'm damn careful using that word nowadays." He stretched the great length of him in a platform rocker, his moccasined feet toward the fire. He had changed his boots but not his jodhpurs. "Where are you staying, Mrs. Osborn? May I call you Kate? I remember that byline from Chicago."

"Please do. I'm staying in Venice."

"Why?"

"It seemed more central to your interests than most places."

"That's real perceptive of you. The university is my big interest nowadays. I'm not a great book man, you understand . . ." He glanced about his own library, his eyes resting now and then on a title. "You know what I like, Kate? Speeches. Or as they used to call them, o-rations . . . Clay, Calhoun, and Lincoln. Even Steve Douglas, that Everett Dirksen of his day."

Laurie came in, having changed into skirt and sweater. She poured herself a light whiskey. A welt of waistline fat showed faintly beneath the wool.

"The university—I don't think it's any the worse for my taking a hand. Wouldn't you say that was the consensus over there, Laurie?"

"In most quarters."

"I don't care about the ones I'm not the consensus in," he said. "Like most schools, it's in transition. I'm all for the kids in this area. Some other areas—that's something else. But, hell, there was more damn nonsense being taught in that school a few years ago: the State University at Shangri-la: that's about how relevant it was. We've got a lot of scholarship kids, and they come from working people, from the mines, some of them. And the blacks: to look at them, you'd think they came from Zanzibar, but they're from southern Illinois and proud of it. Do you know anybody over there, Kate?"

"I came down in the train from Chicago with a Professor Forbes of the physics department."

Higgins turned to Laurie, who had settled on the sofa, which was centered between his chair and mine. "Forbes?" he asked.

"Lowenthal," she said.

Higgins grunted and took a sip of whiskey.

"I found him both articulate and informative," I said. It was not hard now to guess their disparate approaches to science.

"About what?" He was skeptical and not really interested.

"He explained how energy is converted into electric power." I could not resist adding: "The Soviets seem to have come up with a direct converter that puts them two or three years ahead of us."

"That's the Lowenthal gang, all right," he said, as though reassured. "The Russians are coming, the Russians are coming. For years that was how they got their own way, and subsidy after subsidy."

"And now that the Russians have passed us," I said blandly, "do you find it a kind of relief?"

"Hell, no. I just don't believe they've passed us. What's this converter thing he's talking about?"

"A direct converter from energy into power. As I understand it, we use nuclear fission to make steam, which in turn makes electricity. They've taken out the steam." I was somewhat aware that in my phrasing of words I came close to baiting him. It did me small honor in my business, and even less service, if he became aware of it.

And Higgins was no fool. Almost at once he said: "That would eliminate a major pollutant. Laurie, get

Bourke on the phone. See if he can come out for lunch." He looked at his watch. "I'll send the copter for him."

While Laurie put through the call, Higgins explained that Hugh Bourke was dean of the newly reorganized School of Science and Engineering. "They're all meshed together now. I don't like an elite corps of anything. Most of the big-name physicists moved on when the subsidies dried up. Big names. After Einstein, who have you heard of? I want you to meet Bourke. This man's a comer." He waited to hear the result of Laurie's call.

A library table stood behind the couch, and that was where the phone was. Laurie reported to Higgins while the dean of the School of Science and Engineering held on: "He's speaking at the Farm Bureau luncheon."

"Let me talk to him." Higgins went around to the table where he hoisted one haunch onto it and made himself comfortable. He spoke with a clubhouse camaraderie and with only the faintest suggestion of paternalism. He asked what Bourke had to say to a roomful of bedrock Republicans. He added a little bourbon to his glass from the decanter while he talked, coming to the matter of my presence and my credentials. "I'd like the two of you to get together while she's out here. I'd like her to get the feeling I have for the university into this piece. When could you see her, Hugh?" And after a moment, to me: "How's four-thirty this afternoon?"

Which, of course, was fine.

"Hugh, what's this business about the Russians converting energy straight into electricity? That fellow Forbes was telling her about it on the train."

I find that no matter how I write this, it reads like burlesque. But I felt at the time I was listening to burlesque. No doubt, the feeling owes to my own ignorance of science as well as to the contrast in styles between Higgins and Forbes. They talked, or rather Higgins listened for three or four minutes. Laurie got me another drink.

I thought of asking her how long she had worked for Higgins, but since her position had not been defined to me, it seemed wiser not to. A hard face, I have said of my first impression; it was not that, so much as a controlled face. No one who ever surprised her would have the satisfaction of knowing it.

"Do you live in New York City, Mrs. Osborn?"

"A few miles north."

"When my husband was alive we often went to New York. Do you know about my husband?"

"No."

I didn't think she believed me. I remembered that Higgins had introduced her by her first name only, which I had thought a rudeness of sorts.

"Does the name Muller mean anything to you?"

"It rings a bell," I said. It was a very distant bell.

"He was indicted for embezzlement of state funds fifteen years ago. He hanged himself before the trial."

I sipped my bourbon, saying nothing. I wondered what I was expected to do with such information. Was it part of the Steve Higgins political legend: the boss with a heart bigger than sin?

Laurie explained: "I always tell people like you. That way, nobody's going to catch you up short. I learned the trick from Clint MacDowell, our public relations man. He calls it vaccination."

When Higgins came back to the rocker he said, "You know who first got onto that process, Kate, the Russians are so proud of? Thomas A. Edison. How do you like that?"

I murmured something cheerful.

"Now. Do you want to take me chronologically or psychologically?"

"Both. For example, how did a poor boy from the slums of East Moline manage to acquire an estate of six hundred acres by the time he was twenty-eight years old?"

"Foresight and foreclosure. The year was 1930."

Higgins considered—or claimed to consider—his greatest asset his curiosity. He had got into one after another of his enterprises because he wanted to know how it worked. "And that goes for my first, and I might say my only, illegal adventure: bootlegging. Not only was I a bootlegger, Kate: I put my ill-gotten gains into the manufacture itself. And with the crash in 1929, and the salvation of any number of people dependent on the repeal of the Eighteenth Amendment, I sold out to a name famous in the making of bourbon long before the ladies in pantaloons sacrificed the thirst of a nation to their own thirst for power. You were asking roundabout where the money came from to buy The Hermitage. That's where it came from.

"I had the Irishman's hunger for land, Kate, and this great chunk of it at that time would have ruined the digestion of a weaker man. You'll remember hearing, at least, of the dust and the drought, and the dumping of milk because there wasn't the price of feeding the cows to be made out of it? Land-hungry and land-poor: there's a combination for you. I became a great follower of the New Deal. In fact, I did a term in Washington learning the gospel of the AAA. I came home and put into practice all that I preached. I plowed under a hundred acres of cotton, the whole of the wheat crop I'd inherited with the land. I dried up the milch cows early, I slaughtered and buried the pigs —and I sat at night with a shotgun across my knees because my neighbors threatened to kill me.

"My own father who had brought me in his arms from Ireland when I was three years old, he would have disowned me if he could have afforded to do it. He said there was no record like it in history for immorality, with the possible exception of the British during the Potato Famine. I remember him sitting of a Sunday afternoon in front of the radio—a Crosley, with the speaker on top, you know?—and listening to Father Coughlin. 'Hit them again, Father! Hit them again!' I can remember the smell of sawdust with him in the room. He was an iceman, and he had great bulging muscles in his arms and shoulders, and his back kept getting more and more stooped. When he died, I had no feeling for him, dead or alive, until I went in the back room with the undertaker—he'd always said he wanted a plain box but a high hill to lie on—and I caught a whiff of fresh wood. The grief came over me then like a torrent.

"But, you know, Kate, I've come full circle. The farmer in this country has never been the same, and the subsidies collected today by some of these rich s.o.b.'s—including myself—cry out for a reckoning."

This was Steve Higgins at his best, brushing up his memories with a touch of poetry—conscious of it, but not self-conscious.

I asked him if he had gotten into politics also out of curiosity.

"Every southern Illinoisian is a politician. Listen, Kate, they breed here like they do in Ireland. It's our resistance to colonial status." This was the first jibe at Chicago I had heard; it was not to be the last. "Yes. I'm in politics too because I'm curious. I don't know any apparatus as complicated as the human being. Or, for that matter, as simple, once you get the hang of him."

At lunch twenty people sat down together, aides of Higgins and their conferees. Laurie said it was like that every day, and indeed from the dining-room window I could see the sweep of field and the windsocks to direct the arrival and departures of private planes. Laurie presided at one end of the table, and it was to her I addressed my compliments on the meal. Higgins himself took me on a tour of the kitchens afterward.

When we were arranging the next session, he asked if I was staying at the Mardi Gras. Then: "I don't suppose you'd like to move into my suite there?"

"Thank you, but I'm perfectly comfortable."

"It's better," he agreed. "I keep it for this and that."

"And a tax deduction," Laurie said.

"And a tax deduction," he repeated, grinning. "You're welcome to stay here if you like. There's room galore in the lodge, and you like the cooking."

"Thank you, Mr. Higgins, but I need . . . perspective." Nor was I yet able to call him by his first name. "I want to be sure of my questions."

"Just be sure, young lady, you get the answers the

way I give them to you and that your boss doesn't make a porridge of them to suit his own appetite."

I weighed those words all afternoon. Were they said in resentment of my having turned down his hospitality—or my slow entry into the familiar address? No. I decided the words were simply the blunt instrument of authority used in the manner to which he was accustomed. To have resented my turning him down suggested sensibilities he could not afford, and probably couldn't tolerate in others. The same attitude would hold in our discussion of Forbes and the Russian converter: it would not have mattered to him whether I thought I was baiting him or not.

On the way out I stopped to talk a few minutes with the gatekeeper. I was interested in why Higgins needed one. Not only was there a gate; the estate was surrounded by a ten-foot cyclone fence with barbed wire atop that.

"It's the times," the man said, "the terrible times we live in. And I've got the job because I'm not good for much else."

"What happened to your foot?" I asked directly.

"Oh, ma'am, that's a story you ought to get from Steve himself. He tells it better."

"You tell me." I shook a cigarette out of my package for him and one for myself, lighting both of them from the dashboard lighter.

"Well," he said, resting his hand on the car door where I had rolled the window down, "Steve and I used to do a bit of drinking together in the old days, and a bit of traveling 'cross the river down by Cairo. Prohibition, you understand?"

"He told me about that part," I said.

"Well, I was the kid with the gun. A beautiful little thirty-two. One night when we was boozing it up like I said—you never knew how long you were going to have to wait, you see, and it got mighty tiresome— Steve bet me a job for the rest of my life that I couldn't shoot off one of my toes. I shot off three of them and I been working for Steve ever since. I used to exercise the horses, sometimes I chauffeur for him, but mostly I just keep the mischief on the other side of this gate."

"What kind of mischief?" I persisted.

"Black or white or Communist Red. I'm waitin' for 'em." He grinned and patted under his arm where I presumed the thirty-two was holstered.

THREE

Because the university was two miles closer that way, I turned onto Route 32 returning to Venice, and that took me into town through the black ghetto. I learned later that it was called Bakerstown because the central building was an abandoned wholesale bakery. Somehow, rural slums are more terrible than those of the city. There is all that sky, and the feeling of open land—just beyond reach. The houses in Bakerstown were not crowded together, but the land looked lifeless and beaten: frozen mud. The houses were run-down, glassless windows blocked with paper, rags, boards . . . and there were many children, and the smell of coal gas was strong: they burned cheap, dirty coal, which perhaps they bootlegged. I did not know. But there were things I did know about coal and coal mines, among them that the cheapest of the product is often consumed nearest home.

There was a new building in Bakerstown: the Democratic Club, red-bricked and flag-draped, and there was a co-op general store.

I paused in front of the former bakery: it had been converted to a Baptist Mission House, the Reverend Stanley Rhodes, pastor. So read the sign that hung from one arm of a curious cross erected on the patch of lawn. The cross was made of plumbers' pipes and joints, I realized, and that seemed too ironic, for with all the outdoor privies I had noticed there could not be much plumbing in Bakerstown.

A sheriff's car cruised by and the driver, bare-headed, motioned to me with a jerk of his thumb to move on. The blue helmet, lying in the back window of the car, brought almost into focus the elusive some-thing connecting the university at Venice, Higgins, and the ghetto. I had an hour I could spend in the library if I found my way on campus without too much diffi-culty.

Large, sprawling, the school had quadrupled its enrollment after World War II and seemed to have simply pushed out into the prairie whenever it needed more space. The architecture was a hodgepodge, from neo-Gothic to Frank Lloyd Wright to Buckminster Fuller. The students were universally casual in dress. Rampant democracy. Except for one characteristic: the very significant presence of campus police.

I did my reading hurriedly in the Douglas Library file of the *Downstate Independent*, the local daily newspaper and a Higgins enterprise. The story I had half-remembered was the campus disturbance at Ven-ice following the Kent State and Mississippi killings.

The violence here had spilled from the campus into the ghetto, with the student militants agitating among the blacks. Sheriff John J. O'Malley of Venice County had moved in with his special deputies, called Blue Hats, and occupied the campus, virtually isolating it from the town. They had also ringed the ghetto.

There was an editorial signed by Steve Higgins himself a week later on the university's right to self-discipline. The Blue Hats were withdrawn and the campus police force doubled.

I asked a student-librarian if there had been any aftermath. "Not on campus, really," he said. "But in Bakerstown there's still sniping, and the Blue Hats take potshots now and then—just to keep things even."

❖   ❖   ❖

The Science Administration Building was at the end of a rectangular park, a modern brick building with a first-floor facade entirely of glass. Approaching, you could see the comings and goings among the offices as though they opened on the outdoors itself—an eerie, stagelike effect. I signed in at four-thirty only to have a guard rush up and tell me that it was not necessary to sign in until after eight P.M. I crossed out my name and went along the corridor to Dean Bourke's office.

He came around his desk and shook hands. He did not have much hair left, and he had never had much chin. A chunkily built man, slightly hunched, and with a habit of puffing his cheeks, his resemblance to a bullfrog would be readily discovered by every batch of undergraduates. I started with sympathy. His frankness about his own situation at Venice State was such that right off I liked him.

"You can imagine how I felt coming into this job —an outsider, a nonacademician, a mere M.S. and that in business administration, you might say the appointee of a politician . . . and on top of that I was expected to chase the saints out of paradise—to break up the physics department. It was time, we figured, to be relevant and that meant turning our resources to a cure for the sick man of industry, coal . . ."

He took me on a tour of Exhibition Hall in which there were the plans and the models of machines and their processes in dusting coal. When we returned to his office, Bourke spoke again of the physics department. "You must understand, Mrs. Osborn, the shift in emphasis does not mean that we are blind to the merits of basic research. It is simply the philosophy of this administration to find out what to do with that which we already know. Just what you've stirred up with this clean-heat business, I don't know. It will be interesting to find out. Would you like to meet Professor Lowenthal, by the way?"

"I would very much like to meet him," I said.

He telephoned upstairs. The line was busy, and waiting, he spoke of the experiment Lowenthal and Forbes had commenced the previous summer at a West Coast laboratory. "We've dismantled our own cyclotron."

"So I heard."

"Even if we hadn't, they needed more energy than ours was able to generate. Who knows? Papa keeps saying, We may yet come up with something *you* will find useful. I am not a villain to him: I am merely someone waiting for the jackpot every time he pulls the lever. Forbes told you about the grant from the Reiss Foundation?"

I nodded.

"Papa is very proud of him. It has become a habit among all of us to call Lowenthal 'Papa.' I hardly know when I do it myself."

The phone was still busy when he tried it again, so we went upstairs without announcing ourselves. Professor Lowenthal had already left for the day. We spoke for a few minutes with Miss Ingrams, his secretary, who wanted Dean Bourke to know—and therefore rather awkwardly made the point—that she was having dinner in the Lowenthal home that night. It was something I came to think about afterward when it became important to understand the attitudes between the town and the university. Miss Ingrams had to be in her sixties and was, I felt sure, native-born.

We were all about to leave the office when Forbes walked in, a sheaf of papers in hand. He looked at me as though uncertain whether he wanted to see me or not. Miss Ingrams took one look at the handful of papers and scurried out of the room. It was so obvious an escape the men and I laughed.

"I shouldn't laugh," Forbes said. "She's left me to do my two-fingered exercise."

"As long as he can read it," the dean said.

"He *can* read, can't he?" Forbes said, and so I knew he was speaking of Higgins.

Dean Bourke sighed and looked at his watch.

I said to Forbes: "I got you into something, didn't I?"

"My dear woman, you have no idea." Then he melted. He offered me his hand and said, "Hello again."

"Hospitality will get you nowhere," I said. "I don't type any better than you do."

They laughed and the dean decided he could leave Forbes and me in one another's company.

"I'm sorry if I was rude on the train," Forbes said in the wake of Bourke's departure. "You gave me a nasty turn with the Higgins hook-up."

"I can understand it now. I'm sorry about this . . ." I pointed to the papers in his hand.

"It's all right. I'm a bit too high to do anything else these days anyway." He folded the papers and put them in his pocket. "Look, do you like to walk?"

"An Englishman asked me that once, and I made the mistake of saying yes."

We walked a great part of the campus very much at ease with one another. A long lagoon separated the old campus from the new, which also included faculty housing. A footbridge spanned the lagoon, and at one end there was skating while the other was patchy with water, as it was beneath the bridge. We could see ourselves looking down, and behind the reflections that of the cloud banks. We watched the skaters for a long time. I learned that he had grown up in eastern Canada. I asked him if he had family there.

"My mother's still alive. Very much alive. I don't see her often. We tend to quarrel—except at a distance. She never had any doubt that I was going to be . . . a very particular person."

I looked up at him as he stared ahead, seemingly to where several skaters were building a fire on the near bank. It was a graying twilight and his eyes looked dark, almost purple.

"And?"

"And of course I am," he said mockingly. Then: "I write her often. I make things up for her, achievements, honors, you know. I exaggerate."

"Which of us doesn't, writing home?" I said.

"At forty-five?"

"At sixty. Especially if we started it at sixteen," I said.

A pair of skaters glided toward us, and the way they hugged one another seemed to suggest that everybody should. Nearing the warning sign they clove the ice in the abruptness of their turnabout.

"She hates Lowenthal, you see," he said, staring ahead still. "She thinks he uses me, that he has always used me. Which isn't true in any way, shape, or form. So, I counterattack. You're right. It is behavior left over from adolescence, but I don't seem able to help myself."

"What will she say about the foundation grant?"

"She'll say . . . 'Reiss—isn't that another Jewish name?' "

"I see," I murmured, and what seemed evident to me was that Mrs. Forbes did not believe her son to be worthy of his mother. "But Dean Bourke says 'Papa' is very proud of you."

"Papa—I don't call him that, you know. Everybody else does. Yes. Papa, the dean, I daresay even Higgins knows my name today." I did not say how close he came to calling his hitherto anonymous status with Higgins. He turned his head and bent a little lower, for I am not very tall. There was something wild in his eyes as he looked into mine, angry. "And will you tell me, Katherine Osborn, in what manner I have changed from what I was yesterday morning?"

"I did not know you yesterday morning," I said.

"And do you think you know me now?"

"I would not presume to say that. I know a little about someone now whom I knew nothing at all about before yesterday afternoon. I would say no more than that."

"Say Randall," he said.

"Randall."

"You have such nice eyes. And you are a good writer."

"How do you know that?"

"Bourke gave me a reprint of your story on the mine disaster."

"I'm flattered," I said quietly.

"So ought to be that bastard, Higgins. Do you like him?"

I countered with a question of my own. "Haven't you ever met him?"

"Good God, no. And I'll be honest about it: I'd like to. I think I'd like the way he lives."

He walked me back to where I had parked the car. I offered to drive him home, and he offered to buy me a drink at the nearest respectable bar. We did neither, for although he referred acidly to the "diplomatic pouch" in which he had to have his précis for Higgins by morning, we both understood that he wanted very much to have it perfect.

FOUR

I awoke to the persistent wail of sirens. It was twenty minutes to six with no sign yet of dawn. There was no reason I had to respond, except that if I hadn't, I belonged in another profession.

On Main Street I turned in behind two cars streaking through the town with their lights flashing bright to dim to bright to dim. I followed them through the campus gates and on to where the police cars, marked and unmarked, were converging. It was the mall in front of the Science Administration Building. Men, fastening their blue helmets as they ran, gathered in that curiously transparent lobby; on the steps the campus police blocked the entry to all civilians. My press identification got me nowhere. No one would say what had happened; they did not even seem to be asking one another.

I drifted back to the sidewalk. There was an acrid

smell in the air, faintly familiar, and a haze that bleared the revolving red lights in the police-car bubbles. The effect was psychedelic. I spoke to a young man who got off a bicycle beside me. Long hair and a beard. I asked him what the odd smell was.

"The incinerator. We're on the windward side today. What's up, do you know?"

"No."

"Like maggots swarming, aren't they?"

And indeed the lobby lights did give the blue hats an eerie luminosity, a disembodied busyness.

The time of day suggested that the alarm might have been given by custodial personnel coming on duty. I went looking for a rear entrance to the building. The man with the bicycle caught up with me. He had guessed what I was looking for, and offered to show me the way to a side door. He padlocked his bicycle to a lamppost.

"Are you a science student?" I asked.

"An associate prof in the humanities—such as there are left of them."

We went down a steep path to an entrance below ground level. A light burned over it. My companion was older than I had thought at first glance. Obviously. The beard was flaming red. He tried the door and, finding it locked, rang the bell.

"My name is Gillespie," he said. "I'm generally called Gilly."

"Katherine Osborn," I said.

"I thought I recognized you." I am not all that recognizable, but before he got to an explanation, a man in white coveralls opened the door. Gillespie held up two fingers in the V-sign. "Peace," he said. "What's going on, Olie?"

"I wouldn't do that no more, Gilly," he said, a slow-spoken man. "It's going to get you into trouble."

"Can't we come in?" Gilly said.

"They wouldn't like it." Olie jerked his head, presumably indicating the police.

"_ _ _ they," Gilly said.

Olie shook his head. "I can't let you in. There's something bad happened upstairs. Professor Lowenthal was murdered up there in his office sometime during the night."

"Oh-h-h," Gilly said, a stricken sound.

I asked Gillespie if he knew him.

He nodded. "His son and I run the Arts Theatre."

I don't know which surprised me more, the death or the information that Lowenthal had a son.

"I'm sorry, Gilly," the workman said as Gillespie turned away.

He lifted his hand, a gesture of thanks in which he subconsciously shaped the V again. Without looking round he said: "What time did it happen, Olie?"

"All I know, he signed in at ten-fifteen."

I heard the door close behind us, but when we had gone no more than a few steps it opened again, and a man not afraid to raise his voice in the dark called: "Gilly? What's on your mind?"

We went back. The blue hat shone beneath the light.

"I didn't know till Olie told me," Gilly said. "Chief Deputy Everett, Miss Osborn—of *Saturday Magazine*."

"Chief Special Deputy," Everett corrected.

"There's regulars and there's specials. Was there something you wanted in the building, coming round to the back?" A big, round-faced man, he had trouble trying to look severe, I thought.

I said, "My fault. I wanted to get in as a member of the press."

"The sheriff's going to give a statement in about an hour. We'd've invited you in upstairs, ma'am, if we wanted you."

"All right, Ev. You've made your point. What odds? Look, Chief Special Deputy, do you know a physics graduate student named Alexander Yeager? You ought to talk to him. He and some friends met Papa last night going on ten o'clock. They wanted to use his office for a meeting, but he refused permission."

"Somebody used it, Gilly. Somebody went through it like a hurricane. And some time in there they bashed the poor old fool's head in with a statue that was sitting on his desk. Now you want to know why I'm telling you this, don't you, Gilly? And you, ma'am. Because I think the likes of Gillespie here ought to know it: they left their trademark on his desk up there. After they got all through, they left one great peace symbol right in the middle of his desk."

"That's last year's scene," Gillespie said, and unabashedly wiped his eyes and his nose with the back of his hand.

"I'm telling you what's left of last night's job."

"Okay," Gilly said, and again we started away.

"How do you spell Yeager?" Everett called after him. And when the teacher told him, he said, "I never knew you to be so helpful to the police before."

"Be sure you tell that to Yeager," Gillespie said.

I waited while he unlocked the bicycle chain.

"I feel like a bloody informer," he said.

I said, "Let's have coffee somewhere. I'm not on a newsbeat."

"At my place," Gilly said.

We managed to wedge his bicycle into the trunk with the help of a couple of deputies for whom there seemed no other job at the moment.

Gillespie lived in a squat log building surrounded by trailers. It had been a speakeasy in the 1920s, and during the great mine disaster in the forties, it had served as an interim hospital. The hills, he pointed out, were slag heaps on which the grass was at long last beginning to grow. The trailer camp had sprung up around Gilly himself, improvised housing where students could have a community life in their own style. I noticed the cooperative store and ventured the opinion that the town merchants would take a dim view of it.

"They've got a snake-eyed view of us at best," Gilly said. "It was a great joke at a county supervisors' meeting, according to one of our town elders, quote: They rap together and they crap together, and after that they fornicate." He grinned and threw open the cottage door. "I guess we do a lot of fornicating at that." He called out: "Norah?" and explained that she was a friend who lived with him.

The fragrance of coffee and bacon and the warmth of the house seemed to crawl inside me. There was one very large bedroom-living room-library with books everywhere, even on the unmade bed and tumbling from a stack on the floor beside it. Posters and paintings crowded the walls, mostly on theatrical themes. Among them I spotted a reproduction of one of my favorites,

Picasso's "Acrobats." A large Irish setter unraveled the bedclothes and jumped out to meet us.

"That's Barnaby," Gilly said, and again called out, "Norah?"

"I'm coming, I'm coming."

Barnaby sauntered up. When I gave him no more than a desultory pat, he promptly goosed me.

"He does that once to every customer," Gilly said, and lifted the dog's backside somewhat gently from the floor with the instep of his foot and propelled him back toward the bed.

A tall girl came from the kitchen, her hair in two thick braids, which she tossed over her shoulders. She wore slacks and a blue tunic. She was stunning, blue-eyed and black-haired, Irish as the Dark Kathleen herself. She seemed in no way surprised that Gilly should have brought someone home with him at that hour. I surmised the door was never locked except, possibly, when they were in bed.

"Aren't you cold?" she said. He wore jeans and only a denim jacket, his perpetual garb, I was to learn. He rarely wore a coat, and owned but one suit.

"Of course I'm cold," he said, and then introduced us. Her last name was Fallon. It was hard for him to tell her what had happened. Finally he blurted it out.

Norah sat down, very thoughtful. "Poor Dick," she said.

"Poor everybody. I want to call Alex Yeager."

"What time did it happen?"

"It had to be after ten-fifteen. Would you get us some coffee, love? And I guess we could all use break-fast." While he dialed the phone, he said, "Norah, you know the byline of Katherine Osborn in *Saturday Magazine*."

"Oh, my God," she said.

I must say it felt good for I was thinking of all the things Norah Fallon had going for her.

Gilly got his party and after he exploded: "All right, so I'm a shit," Norah suggested that she and I go into the kitchen while she cooked some eggs to go with the bacon.

I learned that she worked mornings on the advertising layouts for the *Downstate Independent;* in the afternoons she attended classes. She was taking her master's in the history of art. Venice, Illinois, seemed a strange place in which to take that degree, but when she told me that she was working with Gilly and Richard Lowenthal on a wild production of *As You Like It*, I knew she was at Venice because she wanted to be.

Gilly came in and sat down at the kitchen table. "I wish I knew what happened here last night." He glanced at me. "I'll fill you in after breakfast, if you like."

"I suppose I ought to tell you—I'm out here on an assignment. I'm doing a feature on Steve Higgins."

"I didn't think he'd made it yet," Gilly said.

"We haven't scheduled the story either."

Norah said, "What do you mean, hasn't made it yet? He owns an empire. Even I work for him."

Gilly smiled. "That does make him an emperor. What I meant was, there has to be something else— politics, maybe? Philanthropy? Or is he making himself chancellor of the university?"

I asked Norah if she knew Higgins.

"He makes a pass at me now and then."

"He'd be misbegotten if he didn't," I said.

Norah blushed and hurried the bacon and eggs.

Gilly poured the coffee. "I hope you don't get screwed up with Higgins—being here, I mean," he said. "He's got no use for me."

I said, "You'll have to start from the beginning, I'm afraid."

Gilly was slow to choose his point of entry. "It's a labyrinth, you know? . . . Well, there's a slick cat named Hugh Bourke now dean of the School of Science, Mining and Engineering. Higgins got him in a few years ago. It goes like this: Higgins delivers the votes for the governor. The governor appoints the university chancellor, the chancellor appoints the deans, the trustees confirm or contest. Contest, yeah! Now Bourke doesn't know an atom from a bulldozer, but he's a quick study. He was brought in to do a hatchet job anyway. They combined Science with Mining and Engineering. That tells the story right there. And the coal mines. Isn't that *your* specialty?"

"I did a story once," I said. It had won me the big prize in journalism.

"That's what I knew you from," Gilly said. "My father's a coal miner, and both my grandfathers were, and I've been in the mines myself. And that's Bourke's background, too. He came out of the Federal Bureau of Mines to Venice State, and he went into the Bureau of Mines from Venice County. The federal government is Higgins' idea of a finishing school. Anyway, with Bourke in the deanery, the whole emphasis has switched from theory to practice. The physicists lost their heads. Lowenthal was the last of the great theorists at Venice . . ."

I interrupted to ask if Randall Forbes was in that class.

"That's hard to say. You couldn't really tell where he began and Lowenthal left off. Yeager—whom I called a few minutes ago—is doing his doctorate with him and hates it. But I'd say that was Yeager's fault, not Forbes', wouldn't you, Norah?"

"It's nobody's fault. It's the way things are."

"My God, you sound like Siobhan McKenna doing *Riders to the Sea.*"

"That's who I am today," she said crossly.

Gilly grinned. To me: "What's happened recently," he went on, "the University at Venice has come up with a new way to treat coal before it goes on the market, a fantastic percentage of dust removal. But it's from the coal, not from the coal mines. The mines are dirtier than ever and more dangerous, as you know. It takes a lot of money to improve the product, a lot of coal. That means more work, no question. But somebody has to say, at what price to lungs and limbs?

"So we've set up an organization called the Brotherhood for Mine Safety, the BMS. This isn't for the record, mind you, because it's premature, but I'm going to tell you what our long-range purpose is: we want to see the mines nationalized. I don't think that shocks you, does it?"

"No, but I think it would shake up the likes of Steve Higgins pretty badly."

"That doesn't bother me in the slightest. It doesn't even bother me if there's violence. Is a mine explosion less violent than a revolution? Does lung cancer hurt less than a bullet? I look at it this way: the revolution isn't going to cost us any more than one good mine disaster."

Norah looked around from where she was stacking the dishes: a troubled frown.

"But," Gilly went on, "I don't know what happened last night. There was a meeting of the Brotherhood that started at the Students' Union. They felt they were being monitored and moved out. We're paranoid in this town about police-bugging. Then they met Lowenthal and he wouldn't let them use his office, which we'd done before. So they wound up here. I should have been at that meeting, but I'm getting paid by the university and I had to put the production first. I don't know what happened. They seemed in a hell of a hurry *not* to tell me. Or is it my imagination? Norah, is it my imagination?"

Norah came to the table, drying her hands on a paper towel. "Gilly, it's only seven-thirty in the morning."

"They could have done it last night when we got home. There was something funny in the way Yeager acted—and now there's Lowenthal's death . . ."

"Gilly, let the police do it."

"Yeah," he said.

Norah gathered the crumbs from around the toaster in the towel. "I must get ready for work."

Gilly said, "I'll tell you what's getting to me: we've accepted as part of our program more employment of blacks in the mines, right? And there were two blacks here last night, Stanley Rhodes, a Baptist preacher the radicals call an Uncle Tom, and *the* radical of Venice

State, George Canby. That's a lot of black power. It was Canby who led last year's student protest clear across town into the ghetto."

He stopped. Both Norah and I waited, but he just sat staring at the toaster. Finally I said: "You're afraid they'll jump on your boat and sink it."

"Yes, I guess that's it . . . and I don't know how to fight it."

"The liberal dilemma," Norah said.

"Oh, ▬—the liberal dilemma."

"That's how I feel about the *Downstate Independent* this morning, but I'm going to work anyway," Norah said. She asked me if there was anything she could do for me at the newspaper office. There was: I wanted the Lowenthal obituary as soon as possible. Norah promised to deliver me a photocopy to the Mardi Gras. The paper did not come out until midafternoon.

She pulled Gilly's face up by the chin whiskers and kissed him on the mouth. "Do me a favor and lock up the house when you leave."

"Don't you trust Barnaby?" Gilly said.

"Please?"

"Okay."

But when she was gone, he said, "I don't know where the key is. I don't think I ever had one."

"You're lucky you haven't needed it till now," I said, getting up.

"I've been waiting for them to steal Barnaby," he said, and walked me to the door. "The trouble is, they can't afford his habit."

"Eating?"

Gilly grinned and offered me his hand. "As Papa

would have said, Sweet are the uses of adversity. He loved Shakespeare, you know. He used to come and sit through rehearsals. He'd say, It clears my head like music. . . . We shall not see his like again."

"What will happen to Forbes, now that he's gone?"

"He'll die."

He did not seem to want to elaborate, and it was time, in any case, for me to go.

FIVE

I put through a call to Mike Fischer before leaving for The Hermitage. He relieved me of covering the Lowenthal death: he would take the story from the wire services, such feature material as I filed by deadline, and the editorial staff would blend the two and bring out copy in what, around the shop, was known as "Mike's style." I always have to fight acquiring Mike's patina myself. He has never touched my copy. It is simply that he is contagious.

Higgins was watching for me, pacing up and down the terrace. He greeted me with questions I could not answer. I knew no more of the murder than he had heard on the nine-o'clock news.

"Don't you listen for rumors?" he said in final exasperation.

We went indoors and I waited while he sat on a

hall chair and removed his boots. He had taken his morning ride early.

"One thing was obvious on the campus," I said, "the sheriff's deputies."

"Blue Hats or regulars?"

"Both, I suppose, but I'm speaking of the Blue Hats."

"Last year I stood up for the youngsters and we got them off the campus. What I said about an elite corps yesterday? That goes for the police as well." He left his boots by the chair, padded in his stocking feet to the closet, and got his moccasins. He took my arm and steered me along toward the library again. "The peace symbol in blood. That's cold charity, wouldn't you say?" I had not heard that it was in blood.

Laurie joined us in the library. She wore twin sweaters and a double strand of pearls. The pearls were real, gorgeously luminous.

"The Blue Hats are out in force again, Laurie," Higgins said. "O'Malley wasn't supposed to do that on his own."

"Maybe there's something up, in Bakerstown," she said.

"They're on campus, that's what I'm telling you."

Laurie shrugged.

Higgins and I had settled into the same places as on the day before. Again the fire had been lighted, but it was earlier, and instead of whiskey, coffee had been set out. Laurie poured.

I said, "Bakerstown was quiet yesterday afternoon when I drove through there."

"So's a bomb till it goes off." He then gave me his version of what had happened in Venice following

Kent and Mississippi. I did not tell him I had read it in the *Independent*. His account did not vary in substance. "But you know, that set up a situation where the tail wagged the dog: when O'Malley won the fall election by a whopping majority, he took the whole Democratic slate in with him. People who wanted to make sure they voted for him went on the straight ticket. So now you might say, I'm beholden to O'Malley."

Laurie snorted.

Higgins pulled a long face. "What does that mean, Laurie?"

"You know what it means." She brought us both coffee. "When the tail's too long for the size of the dog, you cut it down."

Higgins took his with sugar and cream. "It wouldn't be that simple," he said, and changed the subject. "Kate, what about this fellow Forbes? Do you consider yourself a good judge of people?"

"Only when I'm right," I said.

"Like the rest of us. He did a précis for me, and by God, I'm impressed. I'm even willing to take his word on the three-year gap between us and the Russians. He gave me facts, and the arithmetic in numbers, none of this alphabet-soup deal."

"It didn't take long for it to arrive," I said, wondering how the arrangement worked for what Forbes had facetiously called the "diplomatic pouch."

"It came out with this morning's messenger. I do my university work at breakfast."

"From Dean Bourke's office?"

"That's where the pickup is. Ah, I see. It took O'Malley's okay to get it out of there this morning."

All of which raised a disturbing question: when did Forbes deliver the manuscript to the dean's office?

"Did you know he'd swung a grant from some science foundation?"

"He mentioned it," I said.

"That's something I admire, see, Kate. The new administration practically closed down the theoretical physics setup. Cut their funds to the bone. So Forbes has gone out on his own and got them the money they needed. I'd like to meet the man, but I don't want him getting ideas, you know? People have a way of expecting something if I as much as ask their name. Arrange it for me, Kate."

"How?" I did remember that Forbes had admitted wanting to meet Higgins.

Higgins shrugged. "Come right out and ask him if he'd like to meet me. Most people around there think it's a good idea at some time or other. Say you think you can arrange it. But don't commit me to anything except lunch."

"A good lunch," I said dryly.

"You're pulling my leg," Higgins said. "What's at the back of my mind—we might be able to set up some kind of arrangement between industry and the university for him the way we've done it in coal. I'm dead set against having his kind of research in the university. If we hadn't scattered our shot in the universities all over this country, the Russians wouldn't be three years ahead of us. And there'd be less pollution to worry about with these nuclear reactors. I don't think the town of Venice would stand for their starting up that one of theirs again. How many millions down the drain? And Forbes had to crawl on his belly to some tax-free foundation for three hundred thousand."

I drank my coffee and watched Higgins as he got up and poured himself another cup. I did not say that, in my opinion, Forbes, given his own way, would put the reactor back in service. Or would he? One of the first things I had learned about him was his conflict, not unique among academics: between truth and tenure, self-esteem and self-service. Suddenly I thought of what Gillespie had said would happen to Forbes without Papa.

I asked: "Why did Lowenthal stay on at Venice?"

"You mean after the exodus?" He sat down again and stirred his coffee noisily. "Loyalty. The university stood by him during the exposé of his pink politics. In the days of Joe McCarthy."

"I remember," I said.

"That took guts for a state university."

"Did you know him, Steve?"

"McCarthy or Lowenthal?"

"Lowenthal."

"We had him out here a couple of times—during the transition. We had the chairmen of all science departments. How would you describe him, Laurie?"

"Jewish."

"Of course, but . . . character, personality."

"Just the way you said yourself at the time, Steve: a man with the patience of Job. I think you said he could see an ocean in a cup of tea."

"I did say that. You've got those notes, don't you, Laurie? Kate might find them interesting."

"I told you at the time, I gave them to the FBI two or three weeks ago."

"Did you tell me? I guess you did." To me: "You'd think by this time the old boy would have been scrubbed skinless, but some of the new Reds have been sucking in with him. Not that he's been active at all. Not lately. He was no Dr. Spock. But the fact is, I've been wondering ever since I heard the news this morning if there was a connection. This whole business of atomic heat we've been talking about: there's a radical group on campus organized around the coal miners . . ."

He decided to finish his coffee before going on, and I felt the time was at hand to mention Gilly. I was afraid it would catch up with me later if I didn't. I said, "I met a teacher named Gillespie this morning."

After quite a long pause: "What did you think of him?"

I shrugged, but I said, "I found him charming, opinionated, loaded with information—and possible misinformation. I scratch all around the monument, Steve."

His eyes evaded mine. "Take this," he said to Laurie of the cup and saucer he thrust toward her.

She stretched across without getting up from the couch and could not quite reach them. Higgins simply opened his hand and let them fall. Laurie leaned back on the couch and left the pieces on the floor.

"Opinionated. That's a left-wing bigot, isn't it?" There was a tremor in his voice. His eyes darted at mine and away.

I had not thought to draw his ire by what I considered strongly qualified praise of Gillespie. I said quietly, "That might be somebody's definition. It's not mine."

"I mean if you're right-wing you're a bigot. If you're left, you're opinionated. What I'm saying is, I've read enough of *Saturday Magazine* to know their slant: I figure they're planning to put me and the mayor of Chicago in harness, a pair of oxen maybe. Here's the caption for you: out of date, out of touch, out of everything but pocket. Hah! You could go home now. I've just written the piece for you."

"Do you want me to go home now?" I said, and indeed Mike's "battle of the dinosaurs" was very vivid in my mind.

"No. I subscribe to the theory that anything is better than nothing in the way of publicity. Also . . . they sent *you* out here, not one of their gall-and-vinegar fillies."

"Thank you," I said. "And let me reassure you to this extent: I have no intention of writing anything about the mayor of Chicago."

"You don't have to tell me what you're going to write," he said, all but reversing himself. "I believe in freedom of the press." Quicksilver. He rubbed one of his arms above the elbow as he got up from the chair and bent down to pick up the broken china. "Damned horse, he nipped me this morning."

Presently he dropped the pieces into a metal waste basket with a terrible clatter. That seemed to give him further satisfaction. He returned to the rocker completely amiable. "So, Kate. What part of the dynasty are we investigating this morning?"

"Let's do the coal mines since we got off to such a good start on the subject."

He was quite able to grin. Then: "How did you get to Gillespie so soon? Or did he look you up?"

"Neither. We both woke up to the police sirens before dawn. We met in front of the Science Administration Building."

Higgins took his time thinking it over. "A pair of light sleepers," he said, and appeared to dismiss the subject. "Why, Kate, like most of my adventures, I got into the coal-mining business when everybody else was trying to get out."

When I left The Hermitage, shortly before noon that Friday, Higgins' weekend guests were beginning to arrive. We had had to stop because of the noise of the helicopter. I was invited to lunch but I wanted to know how the investigation in Venice was progressing. Higgins wanted it that way too: I was to learn how much he relied on secondary sources in order to evaluate his primary sources. His parting remark: "If you get into any trouble down there, Kate, I've still got a license to practice law in this state."

SIX

Norah Fallon had kept her word: a photocopy of Lowenthal's obituary was waiting for me at the desk when I returned to the hotel. I put it aside until I had written up my notes on that day's interview with Higgins. Then over a sandwich and tea in my room, I read it.

Daniel Frankau Lowenthal was among the distinguished émigrés from Hitler's Germany, arriving in the United States in 1937 along with his Danish wife. He had spent four years in Denmark after leaving Leipzig University where he had taken his doctor's degree and had taught for many years. It was for work commenced in Leipzig that he was eventually awarded the Nobel Prize. His wife, the former Louise Thomasin, also a physicist, died in 1960. Professor Lowenthal is survived by a son, Richard, an instructor in English Literature at Venice State University.

Lowenthal started his American career at Columbia University in New York, moving later to the University of Chicago. Although he had no direct role in the Manhattan Project, the first successful fissioning of the atom, like most nuclear physicists at the time, he sensed that it was about to happen. It was only a question of where and how soon. Everyone prayed it would be in America, not in Germany. Neverthless, Lowenthal was among the earliest petitioners against the use of the atom bomb.

He came to the State University at Venice in 1951 and, under the men he soon attracted to the university, Venice had become one of the ten most prestigious schools in High Energy Physics. . . .

I paused on the word "prestigious" and finished my tea. It seems such a phony word. I read on.

Professor Lowenthal was a lifelong devotee of Shakespeare, famous among his colleagues for always having a quotation appropriate to the occasion, and almost always having it slightly wrong. It has been suggested that his mistakes were sometimes made on purpose, to catch the consciousness of those around him.

I forgave the obituarist the word "prestigious." There followed an appraisal of Lowenthal's contribution to modern physics. The article was attributed to Dr. Hugh Bourke, dean of the School of Science and Engineering. I wondered if Forbes had ghosted it for him. I figured Forbes as restless a ghost as Hamlet's father. Yet, what had he been all these years under Lowenthal? Looking again at the dates, I could assume he had studied with him at the University of Chicago: that would reinforce his sense of competence with the trustees of the Reiss Foundation. Reiss was a name prominent in Chicago philanthropy. But why did I feel his sense of competence needed reinforcement? Which led me to wonder how I was going to get him together with Higgins. I was torn: I wanted very much to contact him and offer my sympathy. At the same time I feared it might seem an intrusion, or worse, the ploy of a working member of the press.

When I thought of his failure to mention Richard Lowenthal to me—although in truth we had not spent much time together—still I felt he would now be in deep emotional trouble. Richard's would be considered legitimate grief, Randall's a little obscene. It has been said of me that I would mother a guppy, given half a chance. I wondered if that wasn't what was happening to me with Forbes.

When I got downstairs the bellboy was cutting the string on a bundle of newspapers: the *Downstate Independent* had just been delivered. There was a photograph of Lowenthal on the front page. You saw at once why everyone would call him "Papa": a benign, white-haired man who looked as though he had taken off his glasses just before the click of the camera. Guessing at his occupation, I would have said he played cello. I sat in the car and read the story. It was headlined: *Famous Physicist Murdered in Campus Office*. In the back of my notebook I synopsized it as follows:

1. Death between 10:30 and midnight from one of several blows about head with bronze statuette.

2. Dinner with son, Richard, and secretary, Miss Teresa Ingrams, at home. Served by Lowenthal housekeeper, Mrs. Grace Gordoni.
3. Walked Miss Ingrams home, cross-campus, around 10 P.M. (fifteen-minute walk—passing within three blocks of Science Administration Building).
4. Met student, Alexander Yeager, and four or five others near Student Union Building. Others not recognized by Ingrams. Spoke apart with Yeager at latter's request. Returned. Said nothing of it. Or of obscenity from one of group.
5. No mention to her of intention to stop at office. Signed in the building at 10:15 P.M.
6. Body discovered 5:15 by Peter Rasmusson, foreman of cleaning crew.
7. About 9 P.M. Richard drove Mrs. Gordoni to Bakerstown. Went on to Arts Center for play rehearsal. There until midnight. Assumed father in bed until call from sheriff's office at 5:30 A.M.
8. Lowenthal spent afternoon with Dean Bourke and J. R. Forbes discussing future of physics department, feasibility of resuming major research.

COMMENTS:

Bourke: "He seemed cheerful, very cooperative, planning reliance on Forbes."

Forbes: "He seemed low in spirits—the cheerfulness was very surface, the front he always put on outside family."

Richard (of father at dinner): "He was

preoccupied, then loquacious. When he did talk I got the feeling of double meanings. I mentioned it. 'Think it but a whim, a toy in blood. . . .' He was back at Shakespeare and I felt better."

Miss Ingrams: "He seemed perfectly normal. But now I think if things had been all right, he'd have mentioned stopping at the office on the way home."

Mrs. Gordoni: "Something he said to me in the kitchen: 'What I like about you, Mrs. Gordoni, when you make a stew, you call it a stew.'"

9. Peace symbol in blood on desk, probably done with typewriter brush. (Fingerprints not collated yet.)
10. O'Malley on state of investigation: proceeding along several lines. Most obvious: Lowenthal surprised person or persons in act of vandalizing office.
   (Building always locked after 8 P.M. but twenty staff members have keys. Entrance through basement also possible. Campus police checked building door hourly throughout night. Nothing irregular. Corridor lights burn regularly till custodial turnoff—5 A.M. Light in Lowenthal office still burning when Rasmusson opened door. Unlocked.)

I glanced through the obituary, thinking that I needn't have troubled Norah for special attention. It seemed to read like the copy she had left me, and yet there was something different. I reread it carefully, too curious not to pursue but reluctant to trudge back into the hotel and upstairs for the photocopy. The difference would not surface for me and I knew it would bother me the rest of the afternoon. So I went back.

To discover a man in my room. He had moved the bed away from the wall and was working at the baseboard. I immediately suspected he was installing a listening device. But he got to his feet, apologized if he had frightened me, and pocketed his tools. He showed identification: Edward Kovac, an employee of Illinois Light and Power. He explained that he was removing all the "spaghetti" in the hotel, supplementary nonprofessional wiring which was illegal.

"Why don't you call the management, ma'am? You'll feel better."

I did call, and while waiting, I looked at the length of wire he handed me. I had myself augmented the lighting outlets in many an apartment with such wire. But those were old buildings. The Mardi Gras wasn't five years old. I said nothing of that to either him or the manager who confirmed his permission to be in the room. The door was supposed to be left open. It had probably blown closed. Probably.

I returned to the car, having forgot what I'd gone back for, thought about Kovac, and then went to a public phone. I looked up his home number and dialed it. A woman answered and I asked to speak to Edward.

"He's on police duty today."

"Isn't there somewhere I can reach him?"

"You can try the sheriff's office. Who's calling him?"

"The Downstate Finance Company," I said, reading from the billboard ad across the street.

When I hung up, I decided it was as good a time as any to present my credentials to Sheriff John J. O'Malley himself.

*　*　*

The county building was one of those great lumps of stone put up at the turn of the century. Three stories high, it housed all the county offices, the records, and the jail as well. The sheriff's office, Operations Section, and jail occupied most of the ground floor with its main entrance at the back of the building. In the parking lot were the state police laboratory truck and several official state cars.

I would not have been surprised if the sheriff had refused to see me, but he asked that I wait until he came out of a meeting in the medical examiner's office. His own office, and indeed the entire Operations Section, despite its modern equipment, had the look and the feel of the days when law enforcement was a more personal pursuit. I mentioned this to the deputy on the desk.

"We still have some of the old traditions," he said. "For example, Mrs. O'Malley cooks for the prisoners and gets a per diem for it. They got an apartment built on last fall and live right on the premises, the sheriff and his wife. The regulars, like myself, are professional police officers—career men, you might say—but the irregulars, the specials, they have the flavor of the old vigilante. Mind, they train in the state police school two weeks a year, and the sheriff keeps them in pretty good shape—calisthenics, target practice, the works. We got one enemy, ma'am. Mind now, this is only a personal point of view—a little old four-letter word."

I must have looked shocked. Which was exactly the effect he wanted. His solemn face opened into a broad smile.

"Beer."

I asked the number of regulars and special deputies.

"The force numbers twenty-four plus clerical help, of course. The specials probably go up to a hundred. They're volunteer, they don't get paid, and they're kind of like—well, you've heard it said—more Catholic than the pope? Some of them are like that. Me, I'm glad to go home when I get off duty, take my shoes off, and forget it, but most of those fellows hang around panting for action."

"Why don't they become professional police then?"

"It's a good question, ma'am. I wonder why they don't."

A few minutes later I met Mrs. O'Malley. She paused at the desk to get that day's voucher countersigned, certifying the number of meals she had served. She was far from the old-fashioned motherly type. Blonde and poutishly pretty, she would be a provocation to confined men, I thought. But, of course, she would not be among them except for trusties who might work in the kitchen. She looked at me with frank curiosity.

The deputy said, "Mrs. Osborn is a reporter. The sheriff said she was to wait."

"John Joseph hasn't had his lunch yet. Are you the writer here to do a story on Steve Higgins?"

"Yes."

"I figured," she said, and then, about to go her way, "Would you like to see my kitchen while you're waiting?"

"I'd love to," I said.

"It's not so much," she said as we moved along the corridor to the door of the jail, "but it's something to do while you're waiting." The bell was sharp and seemed to reverberate through the building. The smell was also sharp: disinfectant, but not quite strong enough to drown the mold and sewage stink.

"I bet Steve was shocked at what happened on campus this morning."

"Yes." What else could I say? I assumed the remark was intended to convey a certain familiarity with Higgins.

The turnkey unlocked the door and we went inside.

It was Mrs. O'Malley who said, "You don't have any weapons on you, do you?"

"Only my pen," I said.

"Maybe you just better leave your purse with Jake, there at the desk, till we come out."

Remembering Kovac, I decided not to. I showed my identification and was allowed to pass, purse and all.

I was aware of standing comparison with Mrs. O'Malley all down the line of officers. I did not think I measured up in quite the ways she did. For once, it didn't trouble me. I was vaguely uneasy at her camaraderie with the men and at the entire absence of women from the staff, even in a clerical capacity.

The kitchen was spotless. It smelled of strong soap and onions. Mrs. O'Malley explained that she did the next day's cooking at night. In the summer it was cooler, and she had just got used to doing it that way. A trusty in prison-fatigues was polishing the aluminum pots. She picked up one already polished and smiled at her reflection in it. The man followed her around the room with his eyes, making no attempt to conceal his covetousness. It made my nerves a little edgy. He was sittting on a stool, a large pot upside down between his knees. What made my nerves a lot edgier was that when we went by him, Mrs. O'Malley put her hand on him, covering his eyes, as she pushed his face away.

"He's a bad boy," she said within his hearing— of a man of at least forty.

I had nothing to say at all.

She invited me to wait for O'Malley in their house, since he could eat his lunch while talking to me.

O'Malley came in with two deputies in attendance. One I recognized as the man named Everett who had come down to the basement of the Administration Building that morning when Gilly and I had been discovered. He said something, leaning close to O'Malley's ear. I suppose he confirmed his recognition of me also. The deputies faded into another room when O'Malley came to meet me. He was clean-cut and lean-bellied. His smile was quick, but his very cold blue eyes took no part in it. His hair was graying, bristle-short, but his complexion and his bone structure were such that he would seem youthful all his life. His whole style was that of a military man, and I suspected he treated his deputies like *aides de camp.* He was a very curious contrast to his floppy, sensuous, easygoing wife.

"There you are," he said. "I was afraid you'd gone and I was going to have to send for you. Better this way."

He motioned me to precede him through the dining room door, and in the room, pulled the chair out from the table alongside the place that had been set for him.

I sat down. "I'd no idea you wanted to see me," I said, defensive in spite of myself. "I came to protest the unauthorized entry—unauthorized by me, at any rate —of one of your men into my hotel room—I strongly suspect for the purpose of setting up a spy post. Why, God knows. Or maybe you do."

"I don't understand. Are you saying you found a listening device in your hotel room?"

"I'm saying I came on one of your men pretending to remove illegal light cord from a room in which there must be twenty electrical outlets."

"Kovac?"

"Kovac."

Mrs. O'Malley brought a chicken pie in a casserole and set it before him. He punctured the crust with several deft stabs of his knife to release the heat.

He looked up at me with a sudden smile. "But, Mrs. Osborn, he is employed by the Electric Company."

I had not expected an admission, but neither had I expected to be so blandly put off.

"Annie, when you bring my dessert, bring Mrs. Osborn some also. And you might bring your notebook. You won't mind giving us a statement, will you?"

"On what?"

"Your association with Andrew Gillespie for one thing. Persons connected with him are under grave suspicion in the murder of Professor Lowenthal. You wouldn't 've known that when you tried to get into the building with him this morning. But what was he doing there? You, I can understand, being a reporter. Was he using you to get in that building himself?"

"Isn't it Gillespie from whom you want the statement, Sheriff?"

"I've already got that, thank you."

I said, "Sheriff, we did not know a murder had been committed when we tried to get in. Your security was perfect."

"So perfect that you sprung it by going round to the back door for your information when you couldn't get it in the front."

I half-laughed, for it was so.

"Did Ed Kovac identify himself as a sheriff's deputy?"

"No."

"But it didn't take you long to find out, did it? On the one hand you're saying we're Gestapo and on the other, you're showing us up for Keystone Cops."

He cut the pie crust in portions and then began the systematic consumption of his lunch. He ate with pistonlike regularity, showing no pleasure in it at all, only concentration.

Mrs. O'Malley brought two portions of Brown Betty and set one before me. The aroma of apple and cinnamon was lovely. She placed a jug of cream between us. "The prisoners get canned milk," she said, "but that's from Steve Higgins' farm."

"You understand, Mrs. Osborn," the sheriff said, "he did not deliver it in person."

"Very funny," his wife said. "My mother and the late Nancy Higgins were friends."

The sheriff finally looked up from his plate. His cold eye rested on his wife's.

"It's the truth, John Joseph."

"It's the truth," he repeated, and put the pudding dish on top of the empty casserole. He ate with the identical motion. I thought to myself: he is a teetotaler, too. And afterward I learned that it was so.

I took a bite of the pudding. Beneath that lovely aroma, there was a distinct flavor of mold in the bread. I pushed it gently from me and when Mrs. O'Malley sat down opposite me with her notebook, I said I was sorry but that I was allergic to cinnamon.

With the same directness that he approached food, the sheriff zeroed in on the BMS, the Brotherhood for Mine Safety, wanting to know what I had learned about them from Gillespie, with particular reference to their meeting at his place the night before.

I had no intention of repeating what Gilly had told me of the background and purpose of the organization. I said that all I knew was what I'd heard him tell Deputy Everett. Indeed I told him very little of what Gilly had spoken to me so openly about: the whole condition of Venice. I have had too much experience being double-talked not to have some little skill at the art myself.

O'Malley, without forewarning, said, "I understand you've been spending some time with Dr. Forbes since you've been in town."

"Very little since I've been in town, Sheriff, an hour's walk on the campus. We did spend a couple of pleasant hours over dinner together on the train."

"Wine and brandy and all that?" It was said with the curl of the lip suggestive to me of a tent evangelist saying the word "concupiscence."

"And all that," I murmured. I'd not have thought Forbes would have been so explicit. Or for that matter that he would have mentioned me at all.

The sheriff sat for a few seconds, thinking. His wife took his spoon and helped herself to the pudding I had set aside. She made a face. "Tastes funny, doesn't it?"

O'Malley pushed his dishes away. "For God's sake, Annie."

She got up and cleared the dishes onto the sideboard.

O'Malley said to me, "You know, of course, that he was out looking for you last night."

I felt a little sick, for I felt sure it was a lie, and therefore had been told in the context of the murder. "I didn't know it," I said.

"At eleven o'clock last night, he asked for you at the desk of the Mardi Gras Inn. He was told you'd gone upstairs early so he went outdoors and looked up at your window to see if the light was on. It wasn't. So he went back in and had a drink by himself and then went home. How does that sound to you?"

It sounded like an attempted alibi, and a very lame one, but I did not want to say so. "I would not have thought him so romantic," I said, and smiled a little.

"Now you know it's funny," the sheriff said, "I

don't think it's all that strange. He's been divorced from his wife, a lonesome sort of life, and all of a sudden a good-looking woman with a glamorous job comes along, has dinner with him, takes a walk with him— he's been working all night on something she got him into. So when he can't unwind, and being a walking man, he goes looking for her. It isn't very often newspaper people go to bed with the chickens." He spread his hands at the reasonableness of it all. "It makes good enough sense to me."

I did not dispute him. It almost made good enough sense to me. Almost.

He got up from the table and gave me a curt little nod. "Why don't you just sit for a minute? Annie can type that up and you can sign it while you're here."

I was not sure what I would be asked to sign. My own feeling was that my most significant testimony was in silences.

The two deputies fell in behind him as he left. Mrs. O'Malley stared after them and drew a deep sigh. "I'll get you a mint to take the taste out of your mouth," she said.

"It's not necessary."

She got up anyway and brought a roll of Lifesavers from the buffet. "I wonder if John Joseph's was moldy too." She laughed silently. "I guess we'll never know. It won't take me long. You can wait in the living room where there's some magazines if you want."

I went into the living room only because I wanted to see it. I wanted to know more about this seemingly institutionalized home. It was like a waiting room outside a doctor's office. Except that the ashtrays had not been emptied since it was last used for a meeting.

There were pictures of interest, however: campaign pictures in which Steve Higgins took the background, looking benignly on a clench-fisted O'Malley.

When Mrs. O'Malley returned and I had signed something that said nothing, really, she seemed reluctant to have me leave. "What's it like at The Hermitage?"

I was surprised that she had not been there, and said so.

"John Joseph always goes alone," she said.

I described the estate. The kitchen especially interested her, an almost childish interest.

"Is there a . . . housekeeper?"

I hesitated, catching an undercurrent. Then I thought, why not dig? It's better than being surprised after publication. I said, "That would be Laurie, I think."

"What's she like?"

"Very efficient."

"I mean . . . you know . . . is she sexy?"

"That's a matter of taste, isn't it? I would say you are sexy. I would not say she is. But that doesn't prove a thing."

She laughed throatily. "It sure doesn't."

Before I left I asked, "How did you know I was doing a story on Higgins?"

"I think Tarkie told me," she said, and when I looked questioningly, added, "He's a deputy. His name is Tarkington."

"And how would he have known?"

I could almost see her closing up, a great blowsy flower pulling itself together at sunset. "I know," she said, "it must've been John Joseph after talking to Dr. Forbes."

Mrs. O'Malley left me at the apartment door where it entered onto the corridor between the wing and the main building. I could have gone out directly from the passageway, but as I was about to step outdoors, I saw a group of young men being herded into the main building by uniformed deputies. I hastened along inside and managed to arrive back at the Operations Section while they were waiting to be booked and fingerprinted. There were five of them, young, defiant-looking, and silent.

As soon as one of the deputies spotted me, he put himself between me and the prisoners, his intention, and a valid one, to shield them from my view. "Don't you know you could louse up the whole judicial process, ma'am?"

"That was not my intention," I said. "Is there a man by the name of Yeager among the group?"

"Here, ma'am!" Very briefly I glimpsed a plumpish young man with heavy glasses.

Two deputies accompanied me to the door.

I called Gilly's number from a public phone in the building and got Norah. I told her that Yeager among several others had been taken into custody by the sheriff.

SEVEN

I was of two minds on whether I wanted to see Randall Forbes or not. My first reaction to the story of his mooning about the Mardi Gras in hopes of seeing me did turn me off. I did not believe it. But of course he would have been there: there would be witnesses. Perhaps that was what he had wanted; that was what was making the story false. He had not wanted to see me, only to be able to say that he was there wanting to see me. The other mind of mine looked at it more kindly: it *was* odd-seeming behavior, and having to explain to O'Malley where he was at that hour and how he came to be there, he had found it more convincing to tell him about the wine we had shared and the walk. . . . The only certainty out of my speculations was that I wanted to think better of him. His remarkable candor, his naiveté, I found endearing . . . oh, God save me, that helpless something. So I returned once more to the campus.

74

In the lobby of the Science Administration Building—that strange, transparent place—I discovered several colleagues of the press waiting to meet with Dean Bourke. Among them was Stu Rosen, an old Chicago friend and drinking partner. He said rumor had it that the FBI had moved into the investigation. It seemed to me that such a step would be automatic, given the nature of Lowenthal's work. I went along with Stu to Bourke's briefing, thinking that Forbes might be there. He wasn't. And when Stu asked the dean what Professor Lowenthal had been working on, Bourke said that the government had requested that the information be kept confidential for the time being. The reporters kept probing at Lowenthal's left-wing associations, to which Bourke always replied that he himself had not been affiliated with the university in those days, and that he did not know of any specific recent affiliations of Lowenthal's. Except the peace movement. "We are all for that, aren't we, gentlemen?"

Afterward Bourke asked me to stay on a few minutes. When we were alone he said, "I'm sorry you did not get to meet him yesterday. We may some day think of him as one of the best things that happened to us here at Venice." He sat, his hands folded beneath his belly, and puffed his cheeks in that froglike manner while he thought over what he was going to say. "It's funny how different the same things look from one day to the next. I can imagine, looking back now on yesterday, that he was preparing—surely not for this—but for some change. He really was pushing Forbes. It might be that he was getting ready to leave us—with Forbes tuned up to take over."

"Don't you want Forbes?" I asked bluntly.

"As a matter of fact, we do. But he doesn't seem to believe it. We want him very much right now."

"Because of the work he and Lowenthal were engaged in?"

"That has something to do with it. But you know, we have no idea whether it's important or not. Neither does the government. I'm not even sure Forbes or Lowenthal himself knew of any special promise in it. But one wants to treat that wavering ego of his with care. I am reminded of a government agency I once worked for. It was the practice to sign all communications with the name of the department head, the subordinate's initials underneath. The time came when the department head moved on. The man who succeeded him signed his own name, of course, but for a long time he kept putting his initials underneath also. We'll just have to see about Forbes."

"The foundation grant should buoy him up."

Bourke grunted assent. "I was wondering if he might panic now, thinking they might withdraw it with Lowenthal's death. I thought of writing them myself and assuring them of our confidence in Forbes, but then I thought that would amount to a gratuitous insult to Forbes. Also, it might be construed by the foundation people as plain greed. We shall just have to see how he shapes up."

"I suppose it's improper of me to ask you if you have any theories on Lowenthal's death?"

"Many—and none. I will not comment on the students who, I understand, have been picked up for interrogation."

"May I ask why not, Dean Bourke?"

He thought about it for a long moment, puffing

and slackening his cheeks. Then: "No comment."

"I think I understand," I said, thinking of the aims and purposes of the BMS.

"Patience is not a characteristic of youth," he said, showing that he understood my understanding. "It was not of my own."

"Do you know where I could find Professor Forbes?"

He looked at his watch and I looked at mine. It was a few minutes before five. He picked up the phone and dialed. Waiting, he said to me, "Remind me of something with Higgins." Then: "Miss Ingrams? Is Forbes still up there with you?"

When he got off the phone, he said, "You can go up and wait for him if you like—unless it's too morbid for you. They've been working for the police since noon, trying to figure out what, if anything, is missing from the files. He's gone across to the Physics Building for a few minutes."

"Higgins," I said, reminding him.

"Yes. Having to practice the art of diplomacy myself so much, I thought it might be useful for you to know about Forbes: he's a great walker, but he also likes to ride horseback. You know what I'm talking about?"

I laughed. "Oh, yes. I'm to introduce him to Higgins by way of a horse. I don't think I should be required to participate in the game at all. But I'll tell that to the big man himself."

"No offense," Bourke said. "Steve likes to ask favors. I think that's useful information when you're dealing with as powerful a man as he is."

"I suppose it's his way of knowing that he's as

powerful a man as he is. I'm grateful to you, Dean Bourke, for giving me so much of your time."

We shook hands across his desk. "A pleasure," he said.

"Did you write the obituary on Lowenthal, by any chance?" I asked while my hand was still in his.

"I didn't even write the epitaph. Forbes should have initialed that. I think he went over the obituary too, probably with young Richard."

Again I thanked him.

"Dinner," he said, letting go of my hand. "Let's say after the funeral. One day early in the week."

   ❊   ❊   ❊

A part of Daniel Lowenthal's office was cordoned off. It included his now-sheeted desk, and the section of floor where the carpeting had been cut out. I saw this in one swift glance as the policeman at the door, this time a campus patrolman, pointed to where Miss Ingrams was working at a table, her back to the room. She turned when I said her name aloud. She was what I must call a traditional spinster—or as they still say in that Southern-oriented part of the state, a maiden lady. Slim, wearing black with a white collar, her graying hair in a bun, she had plainly been crying over her work.

"I can't bear to look," she said of the covered desk. "I see him sitting there, deep, deep, in thought."

"Did you mean it when you said you saw nothing out of the ordinary in his manner yesterday?"

"I didn't really say that, but that's the way the officer put it down, and I couldn't think of how to correct it when I read it over. Sit down, please. Dr. Forbes is generally reliable. The Professor—he could step out for a moment, and the next I'd hear of him would be from Vienna."

"I'll sit there," I said, since she had indicated her own desk and the chair alongside it. I took the desk chair and faced the victim's desk, allowing her to turn her back on it.

"I don't want to talk about it," she said, but having asked me to sit down, she followed suit. "It seems so strange to sit this way! I'm grateful for the last picture I have of him: he was in such good spirits—until we met those dreadful boys. I'm shocked at Yeager. He's one of ours, you know."

"I'm not sure what you mean."

"A Venice boy. It wasn't him who said it. I don't mean he doesn't use bad language, but it was the black one, only I can't prove it."

"What did he say?"

She spelt the word, thrusting her chin out a little: " . . . . . you, Professor."

"Was that because he would not allow them to use this office?"

"I don't know that. Professor Lowenthal did not say one word to me about them. And I don't think he intended to come to the office after he left me or he'd have told me. If he'd done that, you see, I'd have said to go straight on. Land's sake, I've walked home alone many times, and the day it isn't safe for me to do that in Venice . . ." She stopped and turned the thought around to look at it from another angle. "But he'd have said exactly the same thing about stopping at his office, wouldn't he? I can hear him saying it now." She spread her hands and imitated a little shrug, and then the accent: " 'So many times I have done it, Miss Ingrams.' "

She seemed on the verge of tears again, so I digressed for a moment. "I take it you feel perfectly safe on the streets of Venice at night?" I was thinking of the perpetual light.

"Perfectly. But that's thanks to Sheriff O'Malley."

"Do you admire him?"

It was an odd way for me to have phrased a question and may even have seemed naive, for she gave a little "ha?" and thought about it. "Well, now, I believe I do. I've lived in Venice all my life. I remember in the Depression the feeling we had during the miners' strike—a kind of fear that made you sick every time you heard somebody raise his voice, or maybe seeing somebody running on the street. It was real bad. They were bringing the colored boys into town to mine the coal. There's been bad blood ever since, I think. Half the people in Bakerstown—that's the colored section— must be descended from that time. And maybe it's been holding quiet over there right now because some of them remember. We've been afraid of trouble, you know. These veterans coming home and so many of them black, and the drugs. You just don't know. But John O'Malley's doing today exactly what the mayor of Venice did in 1935—that was Joey Harms, Tyler's father. He built up the city police with deputies, and Steve Higgins got a special bill through the state legislature. I think that was his first term . . ."

She paused briefly, the lines in her face not quite as taut. The memory even of a bad time was good, I thought. After all, they had come through in Venice, her people . . . "When you asked me if I admired

John, a funny thing happened: I got a picture of him driving a Ford runabout truck hell-bent for rubber, delivering groceries for Cussacks' Market. He was real serious and determined to get ahead. Then I see him coming home from the Korean War in his captain's uniform and something different in his eyes. My mother was alive then and she used to say, 'John Joseph's seen too much. There's things you don't have to know about in this world, but once you've looked you can't unsee them.' I don't know about that myself. I told it once to Professor Lowenthal and he was shocked. Or pretended to be. He'd go by my desk and shake his finger at me. 'Loo-ook,' he would say, 'look! Never be afraid to look. Lot's wife—like Lady Macbeth, she should have died hereafter.'

"Well, when John Joseph came home, he fell for Annie Ryan. She was pretty in those days; now she's a bit bloomish, but she was hard to beat for looks then. Hard to beat for snootiness, too, but that might've been her mother's doing. They were a little too good for John Joseph the minute he took off that captain's uniform and went back to work at Cussacks'. Annie went with one boy and then another and nothing seemed to come of it. Then all of a sudden she and John Joseph got married after all, and Steve Higgins came down and gave the bride away . . ."

"She told me today that her mother and Mrs. Higgins were good friends," I said.

"Real good friends," Miss Ingrams repeated, her lips fairly curling around the words. There were too many important things I wanted to know to risk turning her off for the sake of gossip that I might not be able to print. And if it was there, it would come out. "I am partial to John. I think the Ryan women laid a trap for him and sprang it when they were ready. I do admire him, but I wouldn't ever 've said it to the Professor. We didn't see eye to eye on some things, him and me."

The phone rang then, a question about the funeral and whether there was to be a memorial. She suggested that they call the Harms' Mortuary or the Lowenthal house, or wait and look in the next day's paper. I would have liked to ask her if she admired Professor Lowenthal, just to see what she would have said. I felt I understood her—in the way of having known two unmarried aunts rather like her when I was young in Illinois. I thought that even if she tried to tell me how she felt about him, she might not have been able to do it, and I wanted to save her that embarrassment. I remembered her concern in letting Dean Bourke know she was to dine with Lowenthal at his home. He belonged in a separate compartment: it was almost a thing of class, and for all that she might have worked on campus most of her life, she was not integrated into the life of the university. She would cling to family or neighborhood friends, some no doubt from childhood. She would feel most at ease at church sociables and she would be as loyal to the *Downstate Independent* as if she wrote its editorials. Which, in a way, she did: they were written for her. These are all concomitants to what I have somewhere called ancestor worship, American-style. But I thought then I understood, as I had not understood before, the commonality of the student rebels with the very poor: they did not have this *cordon sanitaire* between them. *Man, I don't dig this crap.* I felt I did.

"Miss Ingrams," I said when she got off the phone, "supposing Professor Forbes becomes chairman of the department now—mind, I have no knowledge that it's likely to happen, but if it did—would you work for him?"

"The university pays my salary so I work for whoever they say I'm to work for. Professor Lowenthal asked me on the way home last night if I had tenure. I do. I have a pension coming in four years, and if that means working for Dr. Forbes, I certainly will."

I was not sure whether her hostility was directed against Forbes or me. Both, probably. But I might not get the opportunity again so I chanced the big question: "What were they like together—just off the top of your head?"

"Father and son." She looked at me, saying it, and I could see the surprise, the re-examining in its wake.

"I'd have guessed that from talking with Dr. Forbes myself," I reassured her.

"They fought a lot," she said, filling in for herself.

"Over Richard?"

A little sound of recognition. "Yes. . . . In church one Sunday not so long ago—we were reading the parable of the Prodigal Son, and I thought: the elder son —that's Randall Forbes to a tee. He wishes the young one hadn't ever returned." Her expression became quite grave. "I suppose this is gossip we are engaged in, Mrs. Osborn?"

"But isn't it fascinating? How old is Richard?"

"He must be on toward thirty."

"Do you know Andrew Gillespie?"

"Everybody knows Gilly. Crazy Gilly."

"Crazy?"

"It depends on how you look at things. The clothes, the beard, hair he could braid like his ancestors did theirs. And he comes from perfectly normal working people. He's got a sister runs the gift shop on Morgan Street, as nice a girl as you'd want to meet."

"Is she ashamed of him?"

"Oh, no. I don't suppose anybody's ashamed of Gilly. He's just a little crazy. That's all."

She made it sound perfectly plausible, and I thought this was a way of coping . . . with prodigal sons. Only the police took them literally.

I asked her if she had read the account of Lowenthal's last hours in the *Independent*.

"It makes me sound like I was covering up something," she said.

I had not got that impression and I told her so. What I had felt, and still did, was that she fixed things in her mind and in time bolstered them with firm interpretations. She wouldn't be wrong very often, but if she were, it would be damned hard to find the error. It was fortunate that it was not she who was the scientist. "The reason I asked if you'd read it, Miss Ingrams, what did you make of the Professor's remark to his housekeeper: 'When you make a stew, you call it a stew'?"

"I was trying to think, when I read that, what we were talking about when he went out for the ice: it was Dr. Forbes' and the department grant from the Reiss Foundation."

That had been my own conjecture, remembering how I'd felt on the train, the difference in his pitch and his purpose.

"It doesn't look as though he's coming back," I

said, "and I've been firing questions at you like—a reporter."

She managed a little smile. "It's helped me straighten some things out. You could see him at the mortuary tonight. I'm sure he'll show up there."

"It's not important," I murmured. "I'm going to ask you one more question and you mustn't answer it if you think it's too personal: I have the impression that you don't want to work for Dr. Forbes. Why?"

"Because it's hard to know where you stand with him, and I've been around the department for so long, longer than him even. You know what's just occurred to me, Mrs. Osborn—he won't want me. He'll be afraid I'm comparing him with Professor Lowenthal . . ."

When I got up, she also got up. "If he's not coming back," she said, "I'm going home myself. I won't be in this office alone. Not for a long time. Peace . . ." She glanced at the covered desk. "There isn't any such thing as peace in this life. Why can't they understand that, and let people be themselves?"

❖   ❖   ❖

I walked from the Science Administration Building to the Physics Building, passing on the way the octagonal structure of red brick that housed the cyclotron, once the pride of Venice State. All the entrance walks were double barricaded and strung with barbed wire. The KEEP OUT and UNDER PENALTY OF THE LAW signs were prominent.

On the first-floor bulletin board in the Physics Building, I read a poster for the theater production on which Gilly, Norah, and Richard Lowenthal were working. "Escape the pollution of Venice. Come to Arden Forest. The Now Shakespeare."

I had thought I might meet Forbes on the way. But he was not in his office when I inquired. Nor had he taken his classes that day. I did pick up his name in conversation among a group of students. It was in the cafeteria, and it came out of speculation on who would take over from Papa as head of the department.

"Forbes, who else?"

"Oh, man. Now comes the big purge and some rat fink is sure to tell my draft board."

The one girl among them was Forbes' defender.

"You, baby? You'll be the first casualty. A woman physicist? You should be making it in the kitchen."

"Or in bed."

"Not with Forbes!"

Laughter.

❉   ❉   ❉

Outside of the science and engineering complex, there was a distinct air of normalcy. It could have been another campus—or another world. To test my own vibrations, I stopped a boy and girl and asked if they knew about the murder.

"Oh, that's in physics," she said. "We're in the social sciences."

More civilized.

And afterward at a campus cinema where I'd have expected Bergman or Goddard, the double bill consisted of *The Lone Ranger* and *The Return of Sherlock Holmes*.

EIGHT

There were not many mourners at Harms' Mortuary that night. Messages came from around the world, but people stayed away.

"There's something in the air that's bad," Gilly said. "The FBI maybe."

I agreed that the FBI seemed in the air and everywhere these days.

"I can't get near the jail. I'd like to know what's going on. Norah's trying to get the kids a lawyer, someone we can trust. She'll get her father to come down if she has to. He's a lawyer."

"Useful," I murmured.

"The bloody deputies keep saying the kids don't want to see me. If that's the case, I sure as hell want to know it. Kate . . . would you try to see them?"

I agreed to try. "Is that Richard?" I asked of a young man earnestly talking with an older couple and a man who had to be Tyler Harms. I have never known an undertaker who did not look prepared at all times to be taken off himself.

Gilly nodded. "They're discussing where to hide the ashes. The Jewish relatives take a dim view of cremation."

"Not funny, man."

"It's black humor and black is beautiful."

"Are you high, Gilly?"

"No. I wish I were. I'm free-associating—hoping the truth turns up—and ready to turn it down."

"This place is like a period piece," I said of the funeral parlor. The upholstered chairs looked overstuffed, pompous, and hard as horsehair. The unupholstered were upright, plain, and durable. The closed coffin was set far back in the room, banked with ferns and lilies, which fairly drenched us all with their fragrance.

"Late Scott Fitzgerald," Gilly said, "and look at all those rented lilies."

"It's almost Easter."

"I know. I'm working on a pageant with the Mission House in Bakerstown."

By a trailing association of my own, rented Easter lilies, the Easter hunt, Higgins, politics—and a novel about an Irish-American politician who hired a dog for his television appearance, I said, "Is Barnaby a rented dog?"

Gilly grinned. "I would if I could. I can't even rent him for stud."

"I think he's beautiful," I said.

"Five bucks."

I laughed aloud.

Gilly said, "Forgive me, Kate, but you asked for that."

"I know." He had fallen naturally into calling me Kate and I was glad.

Richard Lowenthal turned at the sound of my laughter. A large head, short-sighted eyes, and slightly stooped, he resembled his father. He smiled and made the motion of clapping his hands, a soundless gesture of approval.

"He means it," Gilly said. "He also means that Papa would have approved. The old boy was anything but solemn."

It was at that moment that Forbes arrived, stopping briefly, I thought dramatically, in the alcove to stare into the parlor before taking a backward step to remove his coat and fling it down on a side chair. He was very pale and he seemed in a state of high agitation. Without breaking stride he went straight to Richard and virtually threw himself into the younger man's arms. There was an awkward business between them of patting and pushing, and the small sounds were animalistic. This, certainly, was a Forbes I had not met. Instinctively, Miss Ingrams moved away from them and, having nowhere else to go, toward us. Gilly was looking down, pulling at his nose.

"How un-American," I said—to Gilly only for only he, to my knowledge, would appreciate it. "Doesn't he know big boys don't cry?"

Whatever Forbes said between sobs, Richard's reply was quite audible: "I didn't accuse you, Randall. Who has, for God's sake?"

Forbes groped in his hip pocket, then used his breast pocket handkerchief. "I would kill the bastards with my own hands."

Richard's Adam's apple went down and up. He turned away from Forbes and, like Miss Ingrams, headed our way because there didn't seem to be any place more comfortable to go. Forbes himself plunged toward the coffin as though he had just discovered its meaning of finality.

Gilly said, "He missed his profession. We could use him in the second act."

"It's real enough," Richard said. "I've seen him hit crises before. It's the snob bit—that's the acting."

"How can you be a phony phony?" Gilly said. He then introduced us. Richard had such nice eyes, brown with golden flecks, warm eyes. It felt good, my having looked into too many cold ones in Venice.

I asked, "Gilly, isn't Yeager Forbes' student?"

"Yes. Not a happy one, but his student."

I waited a moment or two and then crossed the room to Forbes. "Good evening, Doctor."

The eyes seemed quite wild—in what?—their eager recognition? "And so we meet again," he said. "It's a pity it took so violent an occasion."

"The violence is past," I said.

"Is it? Do you feel less violent for the death of a good man? Do you feel purged?"

"Do you?" What else could I have said? The words had been thrust upon me by his attack.

His face contorted as he looked down on me. Nor did he seek to hide the quivering of the muscles. "I want to do something, but there is nothing. What *can* I do?"

"Suffer," I said. "That's what grief is about. Then it wears away. But I am sorry for your loss."

He looked at me deeply, questioningly, and then said, "I believe you." He kept looking at me so that I started to move away. "Are you going?" He sounded almost in panic.

"I've promised to try to see the students who are being detained by the police."

"Let me go with you."

"One of them is Alexander Yeager."

"Who would rather see God than me, I'm sure, but I want to come anyway."

As we passed him, Gilly said, "Let me know."

"Here?"

"Or at home."

Forbes started out without his topcoat and went back for it when I reminded him. There was still the actorish quality to his behavior, and it persisted in the car. He kept rubbing his hands together, and working at each finger. Finally he explained: "I keep feeling what they did to my hands. They soaked them in something and scraped under the nails. No, they scraped the nails first . . . Christ! I don't remember."

"The police?"

"Of course."

That seemed to explain his protest to Richard, and since he was that directly under suspicion it explained also his detailed account to O'Malley of his infatuation with me—if it might be called that.

Again I was aware of the garishness of so much light in the town. "I wonder if all this light makes people feel safe?"

"It makes them feel nothing, blind, most of the time, and that's what they want."

"Do you really believe that?"

"Isn't that what tranquilizers are for?"

I could see him quite clearly when I glanced his way, the headlights of an oncoming car picking up the long nose, high forehead, and the thrust chin which somewhat made up for the weak mouth. It was a face I liked, a kind of exposed face that could not conceal suffering if he had wanted to; thus, I thought, the exaggerated physical activity, to call away attention.

"I guess it is," I said of the tranquilizers.

There was a moment of silence, I had thought of ease, but then his hands began to work again, almost punishing one another, and he started to speak by harshly crying out my name. He went on as though there would not be time enough for what he had to say. "Katherine, I haven't told the police the whole truth, even though I wanted to. Last night the Professor called me a little after ten. He asked me to come to his office. I had only just returned from the Administration Building. I'd put my homework in the dean's pouch for Higgins. To come to his office, mind, not his home where I'd been always welcome. We live less than a block apart, you know, and Richard's never home. I started for his office, but I was angry, hurt. He'd done a very bad thing to me. I wonder if you'll understand: he was giving me the brush-off. I don't know any other way to put it. I'd expected him to take the foundation grant in stride. After all, he's been the recipient of several millions in his lifetime, and I thought this modest little sum—I thought it would allow us to finish something we both cared about. Instead, he went bouncing, yes, bouncing into the dean's office. 'Look what Forbes has accomplished.' You would have thought I'd turned up a new particle. A new element! And that whole issue of the Soviet converter. What a coincidence that you should arrive on my life scene at such a time. . . . He used it to ingratiate me with the Establishment. Mind, I left the house to go to him when he called me, but I rehearsed my grievances.

"You've done that, haven't you? Over and over, saying what you'll say on confrontation? But instead of going to him, I decided, No. Just this once, no. And I kept on walking. How often I stopped, about to turn back, but I didn't do it. It was no accident that I wound up at the Mardi Gras. I wanted to keep away from the Science Building, don't you see? I meant him to go home wondering about me, even worried. I did not want to run back and say to him, I am sorry I didn't come at once. And so I went to the bar and had a drink. And I did think about you. You were the strongest thing I could think of to pull myself away. And finally I inquired at the desk if you were in your room, and they told me you had gone up early."

He fell silent with as little warning as he had commenced. I wanted to remember certain things— especially the gratuitous, "Richard's never home." I said, "All the same, you ought to tell the police why he was in the building."

"Why was he there? Do you know? I only know that he called me and asked me to come."

"And obviously it happened many times before?"

"He has got out of a bathtub and called me to come. And then got back in it again until I got there.

And once when I was late, he wrote out the equations on the shower curtain. Everyone will ask, don't you see, why I didn't go last night, when it was so well known that I didn't ever *not* go."

"And you don't know why you didn't?" I glanced at him as we turned into the courthouse square.

"Do you?"

"Might it not be because you *did* get the grant when no one expected that you would?"

"Yes," he said so quietly that I could hardly hear him over the motor. I leaned closer. He raised his voice. "That's how it would have been. Bless you."

"A little psychology," I said, and I distinctly remember adding to myself, can be a dangerous thing.

"Do you know they've taken all my clothes? And my shoes. I haven't a stitch in my closet. Only what I'm wearing."

"They won't keep them for long."

"But I won't ever feel the same about them."

* * *

I parked at the rear of the county building, or the front of it, from the point of view of the sheriff's office and the jail. A number of private cars were parked there, all of them with deputy sheriff shields. There were two official cars. One pulled out and two others pulled in by the time we went inside.

I was sorry to see Special Deputy Everett on duty at the desk when we reached the Operations Section. Somehow I should have liked to start out fresh with the county police. "You've had a long day, Deputy," I said cheerfully.

"Not much longer than you, ma'am. What can I do for you?" To my companion he said, "Good evening, Doctor." Then to both of us, almost an appeal: "Guerin's in charge of the case in the sheriff's absence, and he's gone home for the night. So if whatever it is could wait till morning, that would be much better."

"Professor Forbes and I would like to see the students who are under detention, Mr. Everett."

"Can't be done without the sheriff's authorization."

"That's what we're looking for, Deputy."

He glanced around to see who was on duty. "Why don't you sit down for a few minutes. I'll try and see what the legal situation is."

There was a bench along the wall inside the double door, but both Forbes and I preferred to stand where we could see what was going on. Everett walked down a row of desks to where one of them was occupied and conferred with the regular officer there. The room was very large—it might at one time have served as a courtroom—and was a curious mixture of modern operations, the facsimile machine, for example, with its rapid feedback of information from Springfield or Washington, with barrack-room informality. A card game was going on at one end of a long interrogation table: these were the special deputies on hand by choice or in case of emergency; their blue helmets were stacked on the windowsill behind them. To a man they rose perhaps six inches in their chairs when I looked their way and nodded.

One of them ambled up and introduced himself. "My name is Tarkington, ma'am. Any way I can be of service to you?" It was Tarkington, whom Mrs. O'Malley had mentioned first as telling her I was doing the Higgins story. She had changed it, saying it was her husband told her, but Tarkington had sprung to mind. I wondered if there wasn't a reason. In his thirties, he had a spoiled kind of good looks—no outstanding feature, and a mouth he twisted a lot probably because he wasn't comfortable with it just plain shut.

"I can't think of any way, thank you," I said.

"You're the magazine lady, aren't you?"

"Yes."

"Come on back. The boys would like to meet you."

I said, "This is Dr. Forbes, Mr. Tarkington."

"Tarkie," the deputy said, reaching out a hand to Forbes. "How are you, Doc?"

"I have been better," Forbes answered him literally. He gestured to me to proceed back if I wished to meet "the boys."

Everett was still in consultation with the regular deputy. Tarkington pulled back the American flag where it hung alongside the desk to make it easier for us to pass. So we went back to meet what our guide called "the specials," ten men altogether, some of them watching the game. It suspended with our coming, everyone laying his hand face down on the table. There was no money in sight. Only grimy matchsticks. And each man had his own beer mug, a few fancy enough to call "tankards." I felt in no way ill at ease among them. I have always enjoyed the company of men and my profession is one in which they are by far the majority: and these were the kind of men I grew up knowing, like friends of my father or like the men who worked on the farm and whom my father rigidly maintained to be his peers. One or two might have been under thirty, none over fifty. A couple of days' growth of beard darkened two or three faces, telling only that they were not office workers. Their jackets identified them as special deputies, and they wore flag patches on their sleeves. I don't know how they felt toward me at that moment. I did not feel hostility. In the corner, a few feet away, were two teletype machines, quiet since our arrival. One of them suddenly began rapping away.

"Shut up, Biddie," Tarkington said.

The men all laughed, some too loudly. It was a family joke, probably stale, but the family was giving moral support to one of its own.

Everett came back and said he was going to put a call through to the sheriff. He gestured that we were to stay where we were and somebody gave me a chair. Forbes stayed near me, hoisting his backside on the unused part of the table. He was far more uncomfortable than I was. He said, "Everett runs the hardware store on Main Street."

"He owns it, Doc," Tarkington said.

I said, hoping to put everyone more at ease, "My father once was a deputy sheriff in Lake County."

"Was he!" Everett turned in his tracks to welcome that bit of information, to reinforce my status with the specials, I thought. If that was necessary, I was not quite so easy with them.

A man came out from a side door checking his fly. It was Edward Kovac, the invader of my hotel room. He stopped short, then grinned and nodded. He went behind a group of filing cabinets and drew himself a beer. I heard the gasp of the tap as it opened and closed. "Bring a couple more, Eddie," Tarkington called to him.

One of the men said, "When was it, missus, up in Lake County? I got a cousin ran for county clerk up there on the Democratic ticket a couple of years back."

"He would have lost," I said.

"You better believe it."

"Away back, during the forties."

"Why, ma'am, you couldn't've been born yet," he said gallantly.

Tarkington reached out and picked up a hand of cards from the table and put them in his breast pocket. "It's not that I don't trust you guys, I'd just hate to lose my openers."

"I'm sorry," I said, of having interrupted the game.

"Perfectly all right. I've been known to sit a rabbit out of its hutch, so this won't hang me up a bit."

Kovac brought the beers, and Tarkington introduced his colleagues by first names only. I was not liking him very much: something sneering in his manner. And leering. I ought to have remembered the names, but I didn't. Only Al with the cousin who ran for county clerk. Al was my father's name. And he used to sing: "Say, don't you remember, they called me Al. It was Al all the time. Say, don't you remember, I'm your pal. . . ." I was going to tell them why my father got a badge in the first place: it was hunting season but we were posted, and he wanted to hunt the hunters. It would not have been a good story . . . not with Tarkington who could wait a rabbit out of its hutch.

"Cheers," I said, lifting my glass.

Forbes simply drank.

Kovac was telling how I had come on him in my room where he was removing old extension wires. He didn't blame me for being upset, the drug scene and all that was going on.

Al asked me what part of Lake County I'd come from, and then how a farm girl from Illinois got to be a famous newspaper woman.

"By going east, man, by going east," someone said.

Tarkington said, "Seems like it was a nice farm girl from Illinois went East a couple of years back and got herself blown up in a New York townhouse making bombs."

I did not say that it wasn't known whether she had been working with explosives, only that she died in the explosion. But I was depressed by the association.

"Don't pay any attention to Tarkie, missus," Al said.

"Why should she? Nobody else does."

"Somebody does, Tarkie, somebody does," one of the men said, and clapped Tarkington on the back as he passed him on the way to the men's room. The others laughed. I thought of Mrs. O'Malley.

Everett came back from the desk and said that O'Malley had consented to our seeing the prisoners. "They won't even thank you, Mrs. Osborn, if you was to try to get them out."

"I hope they talk sweeter to you than they do to us," one of the men said.

"They couldn't be any fouler."

"Tell her what they did tonight, Ev," Kovac said.

"They urinated on their supper trays. Didn't touch the food at all, just urinated over it."

Tarkington said, "And now they're on a so-called hunger strike. That's their bellyache, but when it comes to providing them with orange juice, I know what I'd lace it with."

"We merely want to see them," I said. "One of them is a student of Dr. Forbes'."

"God help me," he said.

"We won't hold it against you, Doc."

"I hate them getting the satisfaction . . ." Kovac said. "What makes them so important?"

I asked Everett: "What are they charged with?"

"Suspicion of conspiracy to commit a felony."

"But the felony has already been committed," I said.

"Yes, ma'am. Do you still want to see them?"

"Of course. I don't know whether they're important or not, but I want to see them in case it turns out that they are."

"You see, ma'am, all the police want to know is what they were doing that was so secret they kept moving around town like they had the itch, but all they'll say . . . well, maybe you heard that kind of language before, but I ain't going to say it to you."

"I know," I said. "It's their vernacular."

"And welcome to it."

"All right, little lady," Everett said. "There's one more step first. It depends on whether the boys want to see you. A reporter from *Saturday Magazine*, right?"

"That's fine."

"Jimmie!" he called out to the man on the switchboard. He had the headgear on but he was sitting at a right angle to the board, watching police circuit television: an automobile accident.

Everett picked up the nearest phone and pressed the signal several times. Suddenly the man fluttered into action. Everett instructed him on getting the student prisoners up to the bullpen if they wanted to talk to me. Jimmie looked round his shoulder sheepishly.

The students consented to see me, and I shook hands around the table, Forbes following suit. I did not finish my beer because I saw no sign anywhere of either female presence or accommodation.

Everett walked us through the corridor to the jail door and added a final word of advice: "They got more rights than civility, but don't take any sass from them." He rang the bell and a uniformed guard came with the key and opened the armored door to us. In the small office off the entry he entered our names and the time in the registration book, and then took us down the corridor, turning, however, before we reached the kitchen. I caught a brief glimpse of a lady in white, Mrs. O'Malley, at work. We passed a cloakroom where the street clothes of the prisoners, tagged with names and cell numbers, hung in a cluster almost as though they were alive and waiting. The smell was worse the deeper within the old building we got. I thought of rats, and then of the sewers of Paris, perhaps because above the stench the gentler aroma of onion floated from Mrs. O'Malley's kitchen.

We reached a large, cage-like room, all bars on our side. Inside it there were benches bolted to the walls. The turnkey held us back until a door to our left and up a few steps swung open and the young men filed in. He jerked his thumb, directing them to proceed into the bullpen. They all wore the gray fatigues of the prison. I briefly caught sight of the cells in the block on the other side of the door, the bleak, wire-meshed lightbulbs, and I could hear the hard rock music, top volume, and the shouts of men. The door closed. The turnkey stepped aside and motioned for Forbes and me to enter.

The prisoners' discovery of Forbes was unpleasant; his reaction was to throw up his hands and say that he would leave.

I said, "This is how it goes, gentlemen: Gillespie suggested that I come and see you, and Dr. Forbes wanted to come with me."

"Like you, I'm under suspicion," Forbes said to them as though that were the ultimate recommendation.

"You're not in jail, Doc," Yeager drawled.

"Do you want me to leave?"

"I want you to stay," I said. "Otherwise we both go now."

The boys grumbled but consented to the interview in Forbes' presence. I did not exactly blame them. They had committed themselves without knowing he was there.

"I'll be watching you," the turnkey said, and closed and locked the gate.

"Piss in your eye."

The officer returned the compliment with an obscene gesture and went his way.

I asked: "Has your bail been set?"

"We haven't even been arraigned," one of them said eagerly.

"Isn't that how you want it?"

"Yeah, but it wouldn't do us much good, ma'am, if there wasn't somebody like you," Yeager said. "But there is somebody, so let's rap it out. Do we *like* being here? Hell, no. But do we like the idea they're so scared of us they put us here? Hell, yes."

"Let's start with names—names and ages." I sat down on one of the benches, Forbes on the other. The boys settled cross-legged on the damp cement floor and faced me. I said, "You'll get rheumatism in your behinds."

"Just another pain in the ass."

They were all students. Alexander Yeager was the oldest at twenty-one, their spokesman. Of the six, only four had the coal mines as background. Yeager was one of them. He was a plump, undistinguished-looking young man at first glance. But the thick glasses concealed a lot of what went on behind them.

He started: "It kicks off at the Students' Union about eight-thirty. We'd reserved a room. Naive me— I'd put down our right name—the BMS. We were just getting with it when I realized people were coming in and out. I mean a porter with cups on a tray, then he fiddles with the coffeemaker. Suddenly, you know, I got the message: we were being monitored. Very calm, cool, I arrange to change rooms with a soccer rap down the hall. The same thing: this time it's some intramural pig emptying wastebaskets. I mean, how obvious can you get? So I get hold of the superintendent, and what happens? *We* get kicked out of the place. The excuse he gives, some of us aren't students. We never said we all were. Well, we lost half our attendance with the bug scare. It's wild, ma'am, but you know, the old labor leaders, the union men chickened out. That left about ten of us. Where to go nearby? We're standing there when Professor Lowenthal comes by with Miss America and I get the idea: why not Papa's office? He never said no. Any time you wanted to rap for peace, to use the Xerox, open house. I mean, you'd line up down there signing in and signing out at night: a farce. I know somebody who signed in once John Dillinger—you know, the gangster. Anyway, I ran after Professor Lowenthal and asked him if we could use his office for a couple of hours. 'No, Yeager, I'm afraid not.' Now that just wasn't like him. Was it, Doc?"

Forbes, startled, said, "No, it wasn't."

Yeager kept looking at him for a second or two. I couldn't interpret his meaning. Nevertheless, I didn't like it. The least it was was insolence. Then, Yeager back to me: "So we rapped at Gilly's and if they got him bugged like Gilly thinks they have, they know fucking well they're holding us on gas. But here's how they read it to us: we waited till the Professor came back from seeing Nellie home, followed him, crashed the Administration Building, then got even with him, bashed in his skull and mucked up his office. And the peace symbol: that's not our thing, ma'am, and the local gentry know it. No matter what they say we're charged with, it's that BMS meeting we're being held for. It's like we're after them and they know it. They're more scared of us than they are of the shitty SDS."

The others agreed.

Forbes said, "What is BMS, may I ask?"

"The Brotherhood for Mine Safety."

"But you're a physicist, a theoretical physicist! Not an industrial pimp."

"Right on, Doc," he said, but with a patronizing undertone that made me want to shake him—I think because it made me despair of Forbes' ever overcoming their antipathy.

"And the SDS?" Forbes asked.

"Students for a Democratic Society."

"Oh, that," Forbes said with a withering contempt of his own.

I said, "Who do you mean when you say the local gentry?"

"The mine owners, the union brass, the politicians, Steve Higgins, and—get this, Doc: Dean Bourke, the Bullfrog himself, the biggest industrial pimp in the registry."

"The Bullfrog? What do you call me?" Forbes asked.

"Do you really want to know, Doc?"

"Never mind."

"They aren't going to be able to hold you for long," I said. "Norah Fallon is trying to get you a lawyer. You may get thrown out of here, too."

"Tell her to skip that! What she can do is get it in the *Independent* that we're being held. She can get one of their reporters down here and we'll spill the stuff we rapped last night. It's dynamite. I don't mean to hurt your feelings, ma'am, but it's the local coverage we need."

"Better take what you can get when you get it, or are you in a hurry to go back to your cells?"

"Oh, man! Those stinkholes."

That reminded me. "*Did* you urinate on the supper trays?"

"No, ma'am. They wouldn't empty the pots for us so we poured them out on the trays."

"Pots? Chamber pots?"

"Well, ma'am, chamber buckets," he said with mock gentility. "One reason I want to hang around is so I can defecate usefully."

"You finally held your meeting at Gillespie's," I said. "Who was there besides yourselves?"

Yeager opened his mouth to speak but, without warning, the lights went up to almost blinding intensity where before they had given out about as much light as Orphan Annie's eyes. "What the hell's this all about?"

"Never mind," I said. "Let's get on with the substance of the meeting."

Forbes got up and turned on the ventilator fan. It made a humming noise. "X cancels Y," he said, "in case you're right about the prevalence of bugs." I was surprised at his being aware in that area.

"Right on, Doc." For the first time someone had spoken to him with cordiality.

Yeager said: "We set up a coordinating committee with the blacks, George Canby—the poor people, Reverend Stanley Rhodes—and the Viet vets who aren't going to take any more shit from the Establishment . . ."

Forbes, about to sit down on the bench again, motioned to Yeager to be quiet. He flattened himself against the wall and thus got a wider view of the passageway we had come along. He shielded his eyes from the harsh lights overhead. After a couple of seconds he nodded that someone was there.

"Let's cool it for a while and see what happens," I said. I clocked two minutes of silence on my watch. The youngsters sat with Yoga ease.

I got up and turned off the fan. The quiet was more intense. Only the throb of the rock music from deep within the cellblock. Two minutes more. The distinct sound of a partially repressed belch came from the passageway. One of the boys giggled. A stomach among them rumbled, then another. "No supper," Yeager whispered.

Whoever was in the passageway cleared his throat.

"Is it the turnkey?" I asked aloud.

No answer.

"Rover, red Rover, why don't you come over?" Yeager called out mockingly.

"Okay, wise guy, why not?" Tarkington strolled out of the darkness into the freakish white glare, and after him by a few steps, another, and then another, until there were five of them, including Kovac, but not Al. The light spangled them with the shadows of the bars. "We figured we might as well get in on the first edition. You're talking for the newspapers, aren't you?"

I said, "Does Deputy Everett know you're here?"

"He didn't see no harm in it, ma'am. And we figured you might need protection."

"Oink," one of the boys said.

"Shut up," I snapped. To Yeager I said, "Do you want to go on?"

Yeager shrugged.

A deputy: "Somebody in there said oink. I dare you get up off your ass and come over here and say it."

Three of the boys made the grunting noises now.

It seemed so childish, so deadly childish, the response of grown men to these deliberate provocations. I thought of the way a family quarrel can accelerate, accusation priming accusation, the biting unreason, the last word, the mockery: "This is what his old man pays for college for, so he can learn to oink." "Old man, hell, we pay his college, man. He rides free on the people's taxes." All the boys were grunting now, except Yeager. Yeager took my notebook from me and wrote something in it. Forbes had taken tortoiseshell glasses from his pocket and was staring at the deputies as though he did not believe what was happening. The angrier they got the more they did look like pigs, or so went even my imagination. Three of them were springing up and down as they shouted at the youngsters who simply sat there heaving out rhythmic, periodic grunts.

I wanted to call for the turnkey to come and get us, but I was afraid of having the gate unlocked between these two factions now. The deputies had to be removed first. But how? The dry bad taste in my mouth was fear.

One of the boys leaned back on his haunches, cupped his hands over his mouth, and in a high falsetto gave the traditional hog call at the top of his lungs: "Souie, souie, souie . . ."

Tarkington screamed in, "You son of a bitch!" and then to one of his colleagues, "Go get the key!"

But a couple of minutes later, Everett arrived with a pair of the regular deputies and the turnkey. Some persuasion, some pushing, a few loose swings: slowly, the specials were persuaded back up the passageway. The boys, grinning, crowded the gate to see the show until it passed from view. Their noises now were whistles and catcalls.

I looked at what Yeager had written in my notebook: "The tape recorder at Gilly's."

"You taped the meeting last night, is that it?"

"Yes, ma'am."

"Why didn't you tell Gilly?"

"I wanted to explain to him first. He's going to try to slow us down, he's always preaching a firm foundation. But we're not waiting, no matter what he says. We learned our lesson when the union buddies finked out last night." Yeager was shouting—or at least talking very loudly to me in order to be heard. But his fellow prisoners gradually let up until it was almost quiet.

The voices having gone silent at the far end of the passage too, the turnkey opened the gate. "Come on. Make your music where it's appreciated." He stood back and drew his revolver, using it to direct one and then the other of them out of the bullpen. Forbes and I waited until last. The cellblock door did not open to receive the prisoners as presumably it was supposed to. The turnkey pounded on it and kicked it, shouting: "Wake up in there!"

Forbes and I stood at the fork in the passageway, the boys a few feet to our right, waiting, some of them on the stone steps leading up to the main block, the empty bullpen with its garish lights to our left.

Again the turnkey shouted, and still no one came to the door locked from the other side. But back down the passageway, spilling over one another in their hurry, came Tarkington and Kovac, Everett and, this time, Al among the others.

"Back into the bullpen!" Forbes waved frantically to the boys.

They began to respond, but too late. And now at last they were silent, afraid. Forbes and I tried to block the deputies until the boys could get by. But Tarkington, there first, caught my chin in his hand. "Look, little lady provocateur . . ."

I meant to bat his hand away with mine, but our hands collided, palm to palm, the noise that of a hard slap. Yeager, short-sighted Yeager, who had taken off his glasses and then, because he couldn't see, had to put them on again, chose to stand and fight on that incident, and with him all the foul-mouthed brethren.

Everett and Al got me through the men and back up the passageway. Al went back, but Everett took me out of the jail and as far as the operations room. Several regular deputies ran by us, and an alarm bell began an incessant ringing. The Operations room was empty except for one man on the desk and Jimmie on the switchboard. Everett held his finger up in front of my face, a trembling finger.

"Now, Mrs. Osborn, you get out of here right now. If you don't I'll arrest you myself for inciting to riot."

I looked at my watch. It was 10:20. I wondered if I'd be able to get through to Steve Higgins by phone. It had seemed a joke, his saying he still had a license to practice law if I needed him.

Forbes came out, a deputy with him I didn't recognize. "This guy needs first aid, Ev."

"A lot of people are going to need first aid. And there's going to be trouble in the cellblock. Who turned on that damned alarm? Turn it off."

"Are you all right?" Forbes said to me. He wrapped his hand in his handkerchief.

"Yes." And to Everett: "Am I allowed to make a call to a lawyer from here?"

"If you want me to arrest you first, absolutely. It's your constitutional right."

"Thanks," I said. "Let's go, Doctor."

Everett ordered the man on the switchboard to let

it go and make sure we got to the car. He didn't like taking orders from Everett. He was a professional and he muttered his contempt for weekend cops. The alarm bell shut off while we were on our way out. The silence was blessed—and of brief duration: a rhythmic noise began far within the jail. It started like a throb, a beat, then you knew it was vocal, a chant. Suddenly I had the rhythm: *Sieg heil!* So I knew the boys were back in the cellblock and getting the other prisoners into the spirit, for more voices swelled the volume, then a metallic clanking, as of shoes pounded on iron bars.

"That's the real music," the deputy said. At the car door he saluted me. "Goodnight, ma'am," he said pleasantly.

It had to be ironic.

I stopped at the first public phone booth. The phone was out of order. Forbes suggested that we go on to his place. His hand, bound in a handkerchief, was under his arm. He'd got it caught trying to close the gate to the bullpen. I agreed to his place and he gave me driving directions.

He partly opened the bandage and sucked at the wound. I saw the whites of his eyes. He had caught me looking at him.

He said, "There's something in the taste of blood that's terribly delicious."

"Life," I said. But I shuddered all the same.

*   *   *

Forbes salved his knuckles and I wrapped and tied the gauze around his hand. I warned him that it would stiffen by morning and that he ought to see a doctor as early as possible. I remained in the bed-room-study to use the phone while he went to the kitchen to make us a drink.

It was Laurie who answered the phone after only one ring. Without covering the mouthpiece, she asked Higgins if he wanted to talk to me. I heard nothing more till he came on the phone.

"Yes, Kate?"

I realized halfway through my account of the jail scene that I sounded apologetic. I stopped it. "I'm concerned for the students, Steve. They took one beating, and I wouldn't want them to get another for what's going on there now."

"A couple of bumps on the noggin's a cheap price to pay for national publicity, Kate. I'm shocked at you for being taken in—by who? Gillespie?"

"By a possible story," I said, again defensively.

"By a crusade. The young miners. I don't mind what you tell me, Kate, as long as you know what you're doing yourself. Make sure the story's worth it. As for the brats in jail, you can relieve yourself of that worry. They'll be out of there in another hour, if not sooner. O'Malley's on his way back there now. He just left. How does that make you feel?"

"Better," I said. I had not known till then where O'Malley was.

"Let me tell you this, Kate: there's another aspect to the Lowenthal case. We may break it from here to-morrow. So why don't you come out around noon. Bring Forbes along if you like. What do you say?"

"I'll come," I said.

"And Forbes?"

"I'll ask him."

"That ought to just about do it, you asking him. Where are you now?"

I looked around, idiotically nonplused at his question, and realizing with ridiculous guilt that I was in Forbes' bedroom.

I hesitated for so long that he said, "Never mind. You're a big girl, Kate. Just forget the crusades and remember you're out here to do business with Steve Higgins. Right?"

I said, "Good night, Steve. Thanks for everything," and hung up.

I sat a moment, staring into space, thinking of O'Malley and Higgins exchanging information about me. I did feel a little sheepish. I also felt that possibly I had been overreacting. Then I was angry again, this time at Tarkington. I had gone out of my way to make friends with the Blue Hats, and if I had failed it was because he had been able to convince his colleagues that I was the enemy. That was what made me angry, the sense of futility: *I did feel that I understood those men.* Their attitudes were similar to my own father's. Which, as my mother, God rest her, would have said, only made the cheese more binding.

Forbes came to the door, two drinks on a tray along with a small bowl of crackers and a wedge of cheddar. He set the tray on the desk. "What?" he said, and indicated the phone.

"The boys will be free in an hour or so," I said.

"You do have power."

"No. It was ordained before I got on the phone."

"You are saying Higgins runs the jail as well as everything else?"

"I'm not saying anything really. O'Malley was out there tonight. Something new has developed in the investigation of Lowenthal's death."

He sat down at the desk chair, swiveling it so that he faced me. He held his wounded hand close to him. "Am I to expect a knock on the door any minute, do you think?"

"That wasn't the impression I got. Whatever it is, they expect to break it to the press tomorrow. I'm to be at The Hermitage at noon." I got up and took my own drink from the tray. "Randall, come with me."

"You, too?"

I did not understand at first. Then I remembered his outpouring on how Lowenthal had tried to get him in with Bourke and Higgins. I asked: "Why do you think Lowenthal called you last night? You must have some idea."

"I don't. I don't think about it because I don't want to know." He took his drink and downed half of it, a good stiff Scotch.

"When is the funeral?" I asked.

"It's private. Family only."

"I see. That ought to include you."

"Oughtn't it? But it doesn't," he said between his teeth. His face began to work and his eyes filled up. He got up and went to the window where he looked out. I felt he was again watching my reflection in a window. He drew back and closed the drapes. "What are we doing in here?" He attempted to laugh.

Both of us glanced toward the bed. You could see the place where I'd been sitting while I phoned.

"Are you close to your husband?"

"As close as most. Closer than some."

"Finesse," he said, and smiled.

"I'll take the tray," I said, thinking it was time that we left that room.

"I can manage."

"Then I'll go to the bathroom while I'm here," I said, and waited for him to leave. Inadvertently I opened the closet door. I closed it again at once and moved along to the bathroom through the only other door except the exit. Forbes, going out, had seen but said nothing. In the bathroom I began to shake: that closet was full of clothes whereas he had told me the police had taken every stitch. I washed my hands and face in cold water and put on lipstick with an unsteady hand. When I went out, I was resolved to leave as quickly as possible.

He anticipated. "I lied to you about the police taking my clothes, Katherine." He was standing at the keyboard of a baby grand piano, the only luxury furniture in a most conventional room.

"Why, for God's sake?"

He shrugged. "To gain your attention. Sympathy." He began to finger a melody, Mozart, I thought. I wasn't sure.

"But you already had that."

"I'm never sure, you see. I will go with you tomorrow—if you still want me to."

"Of course."

He came and sat down opposite me, offering crackers and cheese. "Or was it Higgins' idea?"

"Tell me the truth, Randall: which would please you more—if it were Higgins' idea or mine?"

"Yesterday if it were Higgins'. Today, yours."

"That's exactly the way it was," I said.

"Then I'll be welcome on all counts."

I looked toward the piano. "Do you play?"

"Yes, but I just realized how late it is. And I couldn't with my hand. Besides, there's an astrophysicist living next door who can't stand any music except that which the rest of us can't hear."

I laughed, feeling easier with him again, and therefore liking him again.

He said, his eyes quiet on my face, "I think I could fall in love with you, Katherine."

"Would that help?"

"Yes." Said very quietly, then almost running away from the subject: "What time do we leave in the morning, and shall I be at the hotel?"

"About eleven. I can pick you up here just as easily," I said. "Now I must go. I must find Gillespie and tell him that his boys are to be released."

He walked me to the car although I protested. He admitted that his hand was aching. He opened the car door for me and I got in. Before he closed it, he leaned down and kissed me, a chaste kiss although it was on the mouth.

"I could, you know," he said.

I reached up and brushed his cheek with my hand. It was bristly, burning hot. "Tomorrow," I said.

He backed off and closed the door, and then stood in the night's cold wind until after I had lost sight of him in the car mirror.

NINE

I did not know what to do about Forbes. I debated all the way back to the funeral parlor whether to tell Gilly about his bizarre behavior. What did he hope to gain by making me think he was being harassed by the police—or that he was a prime suspect in the death of Lowenthal? It simply had to mean more than an adolescent-like ploy to get attention. I remembered his protests of innocence to Richard, also embarrassingly unnecessary. Could it mean that he was trying to get himself accused? That *would* be masochism.

It was a few minutes past eleven when I reached the mortuary again. The family was leaving. Gilly was on the steps with them when I drove up. He took me up on the offer of a ride home, and once more we put the bicycle in the trunk of the car. I told him what had happened at the jail, about the tape waiting for him at home, and that the boys would soon go free. "But it was crazy mischief, Gilly, the way they taunted one another. Then when the boys were trapped in the passageway . . . It was a bad scene."

"I'm sorry I got you involved."

"A deputy named Tarkington—do you know him, Gilly?"

"He's a mechanic, works at the Chevrolet shop. And he's one of O'Malley's SS men."

"He didn't like me," I said. "Would there be anything between him and Mrs. O'Malley?"

"Well, let's take the whole picture," Gilly said. "If you want the gossip about Higgins. Maybe you'd rather not have that?"

"He expected me to get it, prepared me, in fact. He said I was to judge it for myself."

"He's a cool one," Gilly said. "Then here's how it goes: Mrs. O'Malley—born Anne Ryan—is supposed to have been a very sexy girl. Her mother and Higgins' wife, who's dead now—but you know that—contrived to marry her off early, before she got into trouble. Higgins lent a hand, a political hoist to a young war vet, John Joseph O'Malley. It worked out fine for everybody but Annie. So when Steve decided to take up the slack, as I'd put it in my vulgar fashion, that worked out fine for everyone, including Annie. They used to say around the poolroom, when Steve took his hands off Annie, John Joseph put them back. But things have changed, probably since O'Malley took 80 per cent of the vote last fall. Or maybe it's just that Steve is not as virile as he used to be. Maybe his mistress is enough for him nowadays."

"And back at the jail?"

"Well, it wouldn't surprise me if, while some of the

boys are playing draw poker, Tarkie's been playing stud."

"It's funny. After all the years I've been around, when I think of a law-and-order man, I take for granted that he's simon-pure."

Gilly said, "There are lots of little old ladies around who feel exactly that way, and when election time comes, they vote their souls."

"I forgot my tennis shoes," I said.

"No offense, Kate. Ignorance, but not innocence."

"I somehow feel I've been had," I said.

"That makes two of us," Gilly said. "Let's hear what's on the tape—before they decide to deal me out altogether."

Norah had to move a chair away from the door when Gilly called out to let us in. "What are you afraid of?" he chided.

"*Pookas*," she said, and went back to where her books were spread out on the coffee table. "I don't know the good guys from the bad guys, Gilly."

I knew very well how she felt.

So did Gilly. He said, "There isn't any difference: there's just their side and our side."

"And they've got the money," Norah added.

Gilly went to the tape recorder. "No word yet from Yeager?"

"No. Dad said that overnight in jail wouldn't hurt them. So much the better for their cause, if they're innocent."

"They're about to be sprung," Gilly said. "And if they don't come here, it's damned strange. Norah, last night's meeting is on tape. Do you think you could shorthand it and then make a transcript?"

Gilly played the tape, replaying when Norah asked him to, and identifying the speakers where he could. It was not until we discussed it afterward with Norah's script as guide, that I fairly well understood what was going on.

Norah and I typed simultaneously. I wanted to get my version of the jail scene on paper.

"Punch, ladies, punch," Gilly said, and made us coffee.

The boys had not come by the time we were drinking the coffee. Norah rested and read my notes, then went back to work. Gilly guided me through a lot of rhetoric and some reason. Here is a page I considered both eloquent and relevant. Canby is the black activist, a senior in sociology. Rhodes is the Baptist preacher.

> *Canby:* Now if you cats want to listen to me, I'll lay it out the way I think ought to go. The fucking war—who fought it, man? Three blacks, one hillbilly, and a coal miner. I mean, look at you. Look at me. We're like educated, right? Did we go to Vietnam? Shit, no. We went to college. Now these Viet vets, they got to have jobs or else. Right, Reverend? Or else?
>
> *Rhodes:* They got to have jobs, right.
>
> *Canby:* The reverend, he's not an or-else man. Now what I'm proposing is this: get these black men to go into the mines. No quotas. A Viet vet wants a job, the Establishment owes it to him. Right? And what this means, Yeager—when you get to the revolutionary

stage in your nationalizing the mines, you got young people digging for you. How's that, man—digging? You just know you can't make a revolution with old men or Uncle Toms. You got to know that.

Committee: Right on.

Canby: The man you got to start on is Higgins. He's not only a mine owner, he's a politician, a very sensitive-type citizen, and we're going into an election year.

Yeager: What do you mean—start on Higgins? He'd kill us if he got a chance.

Canby: That's your hang-up. These are vets I'm talking about, patriots, red-white-and-blue blacks. They put country before color. So you're going to find Mr. Higgins will put the squeeze on the union, on his hiring bosses, and he'll soup up the job-training program, because these boys don't want brooms. They want shovels.

Rhodes: And if the white miners won't cooperate, George? Supposing they strike the mines?

Canby: Then everybody's out. Or else everybody's in. Very simple. And there never was a better market for coal than right now. That's true, isn't it, Yeager?

Yeager: Yeah, till they find something better to make heat with.

Rhodes: I came up from Alabama with my father thirty-five years ago because they advertised for black mine workers—

Canby (interrupts): They gave you on-the-job training then all right, didn't they?

Rhodes: What I'm saying is, they used us colored
folk to break a strike and the people of this
town haven't ever forgiven us.
Canby: Forgiveness is shit, man.

When I had finished I returned the copy to Gilly.
He had just finished reading my account of the jail
scene. I said, "Canby is someone I'd like to meet."

"It's what I was afraid of," Gilly said of the tape.
"Not one bloody word about mine safety, and that's
what the movement's about."

"They do seem to have shifted priorities," Norah
said.

"That's the way it goes with the radical young,"
Gilly said thoughtfully. "Not till they blow something
up do they figure out what to do with what's left . . .
More men in the mines, more money for everybody,
and more dust, and the sooner comes disaster. But
we're not ready for it! All the same, I'd hate to see a
split in the BMS now."

He decided to try the home telephone numbers of
a couple of the boys even though it was after midnight.
Norah commented on the jail scene: one word: "Wild."
Then: "I must say Dr. Forbes is the last person I'd
have thought would know what was going on."

"What does that tell you about him, Norah?"

"I don't know exactly. I'm not the world's greatest
authority on Dr. Forbes. But who is? What I mean
is, who cares? No . . . What I really mean is, who
would have known he cared . . . about anything except his own thing. That's something he'd fight for."

When Gilly returned he said: "Nobody's heard
nothin'," and growled about university illiterates. "I'm

122

sure they'll come here," he added, sounding even less sure than before.

We had scrambled eggs and waited, drinking more coffee. We talked of other things, or tried to, my harking back to the pair of youngsters I had stopped on the campus that afternoon who were in the social sciences.

"That's the way it's going now," Norah said. "Caring is passé, except among the radicals."

"But I'm still in love with the caring generation," I said.

"So was Papa," Gilly said. "Which is why I can't understand his refusing Yeager the use of his office. Unless he intended to use it himself."

"Obviously he did," I said. "He was there." I was going to have to tell O'Malley of Forbes' confiding that Lowenthal had called him to come to the office. And if it turned out to be one more of Forbes' neurotic fabrications? I could not allow that to become my problem. But I proposed to make one more attempt in the morning to persuade Forbes to tell it himself.

"You know, we had a grand put-on going with the old man," Gilly said, the memory warm in his eyes. "We were going to build a production of *The Tempest* around him playing Prospero. He went around the department telling everyone, 'I am going to play in Shakespeare. I am following in my son's footsteps.' He did everything but sell tickets, the ham. Then one day: 'Ach, Gilly—it is all off. How would I ever remember all those words?'"

"He was lovable," Norah said.

"Oh, yes. But nobody's fool."

"Somebody's," I said.

Gilly nodded. "Bourke loves to tell that story, by the way. And then in case you don't get it, he will explain: 'Have you any idea the thousands of mathematical equations this man can carry in his head?' He's so bloody impressed."

"I rather liked Bourke," I said, "the little I saw of him."

"That's what he's there for—to be likable. And he didn't even show up at the funeral parlor tonight."

"You don't give any quarter, do you, Gilly?"

"I don't like second-rate minds in first-rate places. They spread a slow contagion that doesn't show up until it's too late."

"Gilly, without bias, what do you think Lowenthal felt about Forbes?"

He grinned. "Me—without bias?" Then he was serious. "The old man took a lot for granted concerning the esteem due himself. Richard once said his father would have killed him if he'd gone into science. No matter how good he was, he would never have been good enough. I think the old man respected Forbes. If there's one area for sure where Forbes is not a phony, it's his science. It's the one place where he can let go. You know—just let go."

"I know. For some people it's the hardest thing in the world. Haven't you ever told an actor to just play himself?"

"That's it," Gilly said. "Do you like him, Kate?"

"There is something," I said, and left it open. Because I could not close it.

I looked at my watch. It was almost two.

"Wait till the two o'clock news," Gilly said. "I'm afraid the only way we're going to hear anything is on the radio." He sounded very dejected. We all took our plates to the kitchen sink, and on the way Norah put her arm around him. I thought of Forbes' kiss—with its graveyard warmth.

We sat at the kitchen table, waiting out the minutes.

Gilly said, "All of a sudden I feel like an old man."

"A dirty old man?" said Norah.

"Not even that."

I said, "I have a feeling that something has happened which we ought to have known would happen all along, only didn't."

Norah said, "I feel that this house has turned into an ark, and the waters have risen all around us."

Gilly said, "I feel we're haunted. This old house has turned back into the speakeasy it was in the twenties, and outside, the revenue men are slowly closing in." He turned on the radio. The time signal came out full blast. He turned it down. The news followed:

> "Southern Illinois is very much in the news this morning. According to a copyrighted story in the East German morning newspapers, Daniel Lowenthal, the Nobel Prize physicist who was found slain in his Venice campus office yesterday morning, had recently accepted an appointment behind the Iron Curtain. The chancellor of the University of Leipzig confirmed that he was expected to take up his duties at Leipzig next September."

We looked at one another, held our tongues, and leaned a little closer to the radio.

> "In this country, the FBI refused comment, except to say that the bureau will probably con-

duct a routine investigation into the nature of the research in which Professor Lowenthal has recently been engaged.

"Reached at his home for comment a few minutes before air time, Hugh Bourke, dean of the School of Science and Engineering at Venice State, said he had been unaware of Lowenthal's intentions, although the professor was within a year of retirement from his post here. Dean Bourke added that while it was unusual for an American scientist to take an assignment within the Soviet bloc, he knew of no law prohibiting it today. He also recalled that Professor Lowenthal commenced his distinguished career in physics at the University of Leipzig over forty years ago, and that he left Germany only on Hitler's rise to power . . ."

During the commercial break, I said that I was quite sure that specific reference to the University of Leipzig had been deleted from the obituary as it appeared in the *Downstate Independent*, although the university had been named in the photocopy Norah gave me.

Gilly said, "Big fucking deal." Then: "I'm pretty sure Richard didn't know. What about Forbes? Eh, what about him now?"

I glanced at him but did not answer.

"The investigation into Lowenthal's death continues under the direction of Venice County Sheriff John J. O'Malley. Six students at Venice State, held on suspicion of complicity, were released from custody just before midnight. They immediately sought admission to Good Samaritan Hospital for treatment of cuts and bruises they said were inflicted on them by special sheriff's deputies.

"All special deputies were suspended by O'Malley, pending investigation of the incident . . ."

Gilly whistled softly, then motioned us all to attend closely.

"Meanwhile, Alexander Yeager, spokesman for the students, charged at a press gathering in the lobby of the hospital that the group had been detained as harassment. They are members of an avowed radical organization called the Brotherhood for Mine Safety . . ."

"Who says 'avowed radical organization'?" Gilly shouted at the radio.

". . . dedicated to the democrasa . . . sorry —democratization of mine employment, and the eventual nationalization of the mining industry. At a meeting last night the Brotherhood set up an alliance with the blacks and with the Poor People's Party under student leader George Canby and the Reverend Stanley Rhodes . . ."

Gilly turned off the radio, but he kept his eyes on it as though it were the enemy. "What incredible mischief. What arrogance."

I said, "What stupidity."

Gilly kept speaking to the radio: "You want to be martyrs. But it's too soon, you idiots!"

"I very much doubt you will ever convince a young person of that," I said. "I must go home."

Barnaby, the dog, was waiting at the door. He slithered out past me when Gilly opened the door. Gilly closed it again for a moment. "What about your friend Forbes in light of the Leipzig information?"

I shook my head. No comment.

"Does he pimp on the side for the FBI?"

That had not specifically occurred to me. I was not sure what kind of sense it would make to me in the cold light of day. I said, "He'd be good material to work on as an informer but I just don't think he's involved that way."

Gilly managed to smile. "I want you on my team, Kate. Loyalty like yours is priceless."

Barnaby was barking.

"Wait till I get my flashlight," Gilly said. "The damned raccoons take the lids off everybody's garbage cans for him."

By the time he returned the dog had stopped barking. I said good night to Norah, and Gilly and I went outdoors. Gilly whistled, but no Barnaby. He threw the beam of the flashlight down the walk toward where I had left the car. It picked up Barnaby sitting on his haunches a few feet from the car. Again Gilly whistled. The dog lifted his head and sent a wolf-howl spiraling into the night's silence. It chilled my soul. Then he got up and trotted toward us as though to be rewarded for a good deed.

Gilly cleared his throat and said matter-of-factly, "Let's leave your car here for the night, Kate. I'll drive you home in Norah's."

TEN

Norah decided to go with us because, Gilly said, trying to make light of it, she did not trust him to drive her aging Volvo. But I remembered that morning—the morning before; the days were telescoping—her asking Gilly to lock the door. Again she asked it as we left the house.

"I don't know where the key is. If you want it locked we'll have to do it from the inside and go out the chimney."

I said, "Gilly, couldn't your dog be . . ."

"Neurotic?" He finished my sentence. "Absolutely. It comes of living with people. There's not a chance in a thousand that anything's wrong with your car, but I'll go over it in daylight and then bring it to you."

"Do you know what to look for?"

"I know the car's anatomy. I used to drag race. In my undergraduate days that was the thing."

"It doesn't seem so long ago," I said.

"Only far away."

I gave him the car keys and at the hotel door said that he was not to hurry in the morning. They drove off and I went wearily inside. The desk man pointed to a prone figure on a lobby sofa. It was Stu Rosen, the Chicago reporter, asleep with an empty glass in his hand. I took the glass from him, pushed him over, and sat down on the side of the sofa.

He opened one eye, then the other. "It's not that I'm checking up on you, Kate, but where in hell have you been?"

"Why?"

"You don't look beat up to me."

"Come on, Stu. No games."

He sat up and took a crumpled package of cigarettes from his pocket. "The kids said the Blue Hats slapped you around. That's why the sheriff had to suspend them."

"Oh, no . . ." I felt a little sick. Stu couldn't get the cigarette out, so I took the package from him and shook out two of them. I also lit them, Stu having the hands of a drinking man.

"Exaggerated?" Stu said.

"Distorted . . . I jerked my head away and batted at his hand. It made a noise."

"What did he have in mind—and who is he?"

"A deputy named Tarkington. I don't know what he had in mind. I didn't want him to touch me, but . . ."

Stu shrugged. "I like the kids' version. You're quibbling again, Kate."

"No, I'm not. *I was not slapped around.*"

"Where was O'Malley when all this happened?"

"He wasn't there," I said. If I'd have told anyone it would have been Stu, but I did not feel it my place, or in my own interests, to mention Higgins. I got up and put the cigarette out. It tasted horrible. "Please, Stu, don't help that story to snowball. He did not strike me. It was an accident."

"If you say so. I've got a fifth of Old Taylor upstairs. Let's have a nightcap."

"Old Taylor," I repeated, thinking of the train and, aloud, although I meant to say it to myself: "Screw nostalgia."

"That's not exactly what I had in mind, but . . . *noblesse oblige.*"

"Give me a rain check on the drink, Stu. Tomorrow is closing day for my rag, and I've got to get something in to Mike."

"*Saturday's* Saturday," Stu said. "What do you do in your shop if you're kosher?"

"Mike gets you a dispensation."

"Not by my rabbi," Stu said.

I was too tired to think of a comeback.

I was very uneasy about the report that I had been assaulted by the Blue Hats. In my room I tried to reach someone at the *Independent* by phone but there was no answer. I had got the phone number from the masthead of the paper. I turned the page to the Lowenthal obituary: I had been right about the omission of the reference to Leipzig. One wanted to know who decided it should be omitted. Before I threw the paper away I picked up the metal wastebasket and examined it, more than half-expecting a bug. Not that I was sure of recognizing one if I saw it. But, of course, the basket was clean.

Ever wider awake, however tired, I turned on the three o'clock news. It had not changed apparently, but this time I heard out Yeager's story to the press. He had responded to a question on whether nationalization of the mines wouldn't lead to socialism: "Absolutely. That's what we want." And then the details of how the confrontation with the Blue Hats had started: "This Mrs. Osborn from *Saturday Magazine?* When one of them slapped her face, man, we blew. Wouldn't you?"

I found myself, like Gilly, wanting to talk to the radio: that's not true! I was disliking Yeager almost as much as I did Tarkington. I called the radio station and asked to speak to someone on the news desk. I got the all-night disc jockey. The two o'clock news was recorded and repeated at three and four A.M. I tried to leave instructions for the five o'clock reporter. The jockey could not have cared less. He wanted me to request a musical disc. I said, "Play 'Melancholy Baby.'"

After that I took two tranquilizers and set the alarm of my travel clock for eight. I slept badly and dreamed of missing a boat because I could not find my shoes. I've not traveled by boat since my honeymoon. I also dreamed of a house of several stories but I could not get from one floor to the next because the stairs broke apart every time I started up them.

I awoke to the sound of a bell and reached for the clock. I turned off the alarm even though I knew it wasn't ringing. Then the phone rang again. At that point I looked at the time: ten past seven. Finally I managed synchronization and answered the telephone.

"Kate? Your car is gone. It's Gilly."

"Gone?"

"Stolen. I've reported it to the police."

"All right," I said. "I'll call the rental agency and report it as soon as they open."

"You need a car, so I'm going to get dressed and bring Norah's over to you . . ."

"It's not necessary . . ." I started to explain.

"Listen, Kate, the black preacher, Stanley Rhodes —do you know who I'm talking about?"

"Yes—he was at the BMS conference."

"Right. He's been shot to death outside the Mission House in Bakerstown."

           ❉   ❉   ❉

I showered, hot and cold, made instant coffee on the wall burner, and did what I thought would be my good deed for the day. I telephoned Stu Rosen and told him of the second murder in Venice in two days.

He said, "You take this one, Kate. I'll take the next."

ELEVEN

Gilly was waiting for me at the side door, Norah's Volvo resting under the portico. It was a very old car. Gilly beckoned me to follow him into the parking lot first. He pointed to a white Chevrolet Impala.

"It looks like it," I said.

"It's yours all right." He showed me the license tag on the key ring I'd given him. "I've been round to the kitchen and I asked at the desk. Nobody saw it come in. An immaculate delivery."

"You've had the keys since I gave them to you?"

He patted the pocket where they had been since he and Norah drove me home. "Let's leave it for now. I still want to go over it."

"We'd better report it," I said.

"I suppose we had better, but if they don't believe us—what?" He opened the door to Norah's car for me and I got in.

"Nevertheless," I said.

When he was behind the wheel, he said, "Do *you* believe me?"

"Of course."

"I wonder why I thought you wouldn't. Is it all right if I go to Bakerstown with you?"

Again I said, "Of course."

Seven-thirty on a Saturday morning. The town was waking up, it seemed to me, in spasms: here and there were small bursts of activity, a repair crew was rigging up under the overhead traffic light on University and Main streets; a bakery truck and two milk wagons moved along as if in convoy. People in the streets seemed hurrying to get indoors. Imagination or fact? Gilly said it was both. The sky was the color of skim milk. I remarked on it.

Gilly said, "Ofay."

I said, a bit testily, "Are you always political?"

"It's better than nothing. You don't hear the sirens wailing for old Stan Rhodes, do you?"

"A good thing, too."

He thought about it. "Maybe."

"How did you hear about it, Gilly?"

"From the municipal police when I called to report your car had been stolen. They're scared. Every time a black man gets killed they go schizoid: they're sad and they're glad." A couple of blocks on, he said, "Yeager's blab to the reporters last night—that just about finishes the Brotherhood. Red socialism. God Almighty, I can see Higgins' editorial right now: Black Power and Red socialism in the mines. Editorial, hell! Headlines."

"Yeager used me for mischief too—whether he believed it or not. He told them Tarkington had slapped my face. That simply did not happen. How do I go about correcting that one, will you tell me?"

He didn't answer. He was dividing his attention between the street ahead and the rearview mirror. I looked back to see two men carrying a door between them. We had reached the part of town where business establishments were thinning out—used car lots, the lumber yard, a corner delicatessen and a housefront beauty parlor. A poorer residential area. We could not be far from Bakerstown.

"They're boarding up," Gilly said.

I realized that to be the meaning of the door the men carried. Closer to Bakerstown people were roping shutters together in front of their store windows.

"Why, the only thing I can think of for you to do, Kate—get yourself a blue hat and wear it. I've got a feeling we're going to have to stand up and be counted in Venice. Or else we'll be counted lying down."

"Has there been violence lately?"

"Sporadically. In modern times it stems from the black boycott of the white-owned stores downtown. They set up the Bakerstown cooperative last summer modeled on the student store near my place. George Canby moved that along mostly, but we all pitched in when he'd allow it. It's ironic now that Stanley Rhodes welcomed the white students' help. The coop's been fire-bombed three times that I know of. Reprisals followed. And sniping. It's been a bad scene straight through."

We approached Bakerstown by way of Main Street, which was Highway 32. Within sight of the old bakery alongside which was the cross made of plumbers' pipes, there were perhaps twenty police and sheriff's men, the regulars, Gilly pointed out, whose caps somewhat resembled miners' headgear: the plastic protection beneath a soft crown. There was not a Blue Hat in sight. I noticed two black officers among the municipal police. The road was now barricaded.

Gilly made a sharp L-turn into a side street. Another L-turn brought us into the ghetto. Women with coats and shawls, some over their nightclothes, were gathering in clusters. As soon as they saw us, they turned their backs. Gilly kept waving to people, but nobody waved back.

"It's bad, Kate. These people know me. I've been working on an Easter pageant with them."

I could not help it; he sounded so personally offended: "They could use a good resurrection right now," I said.

Some children were huddled alongside the curb at the end of the block. As we were about to pass, they straightened up and hurled a barrage of stones and clumps of dirt. A bottle sailed toward the window on my side. I ducked. It cracked the window. The gang, boys and girls no more than twelve years old, turned heel and ran.

Most of the male population was just beginning to turn out. Their first jaunt of the day was to the outhouse. I commented.

"Yeah," Gilly said. "In the summer it smells like the eighteenth century."

He made a sudden turn up over the curb and drove across an open field in which the grass was bumper high. We lurched into a wagon track and within a few yards came to a halt next to the frame building. Gilly pushed open a door that scraped the floor. "This is the way the saints march in," he said.

The voices were a medley of sobs and moans. I felt like an intruder despite Gilly's familiarity with the building. If once it had smelled like a bakery, it now smelled like what it was, a church—that damp prayer-book smell with a slight overlay of sweetness. We were passing beneath the pulpit, a white-and-gold-painted elevated box, toward where everyone was gathered at the rear of the room when the women there began to shriek. Stabbing cries. Five black women confronted O'Malley, and every feint he made toward them, they cried out and moved together.

It was the body on the floor, covered with sheets, that they were protecting. White-coated ambulance attendants waited at the door with the other police. When the women saw us they linked arms and spread themselves to prevent us also from approaching the body. I read hatred and fear in their tear-streaked faces and felt helpless and sick at being there to be so hated and feared. I wanted to say I hurt too.

Gilly said, "Ida, I want to help."

There was no response. It was as though none of them was named Ida.

O'Malley, as pale as the moon in daylight, said, "There's got to be an autopsy. It's the law. We just want the body for a little while, don't you see?"

"No, sir. I don't see. He cold dead, and I ain't going to give him up to no white man to carve up like he was a carcass." The woman broke hands with her friends and, hugging herself, rocked in misery.

"We need the bullet—if it's still in his body."

Another woman: "What for? To put in another black man?"

And another: "Sheriff, it going to take you five more bullets before you take our parson out of here." She pointed to each of her companions and counted aloud.

"We're going to have to take him, woman. Even if it means getting out the National Guard to do it. And that could do everybody harm. You had no right moving him in here in the first place."

The widow raised her head. "No right? Don't you talk to me about no right, Mister Sheriff. Nobody had the right to kill him either, but it got done. Oh, yes, Lord! It got done. Done for good. No more sweet Alleluias from the pulpit there, no more Praise the Lords! You hear me, sisters? No more Glory in the mornings. He lying here, and he ain't getting up no more. Not this morning, not tomorrow, not the morning after."

Amens, I think I heard.

The sheriff: "I swear to all you people, when we find the killer, he won't go free."

A big woman folded her arms, her head high and her hair a tower: "Sisters, he won't go free. Hear?" The motion forward of her body was a kind of insinuation. To O'Malley: "I tell you, white man, our Reverend there, he free. He a lot freer than you white men ever going to be."

The sheriff turned his back and consulted among his men. Gilly moved closer to the women. He spoke to the one nearest him, nodding toward the widow. "Tell Mrs. Rhodes I'm very sorry for her pain. I loved him too."

"She hear you," the woman said, but very coldly.

O'Malley whirled around. "Tell them I've got to view the body, at least, Gillespie. I don't even know that it's a colored man under there."

"Tell them yourself," Gillespie said. He motioned to me that he wanted to leave. But the sheriff, squatting down, edged forward in that position and snatched the sheet off the victim. The women screamed.

From where did he come? I barely saw the streaking, hurtling figure: a near-giant of a black man slashed his way through the deputies, his arms like scissors, his head tossing a wild burst of hair. He caught O'Malley by the collar of his coat. Then, his other hand between the sheriff's buttocks, he lifted him clear off the floor, turned, and set him down among the paralyzed deputies. Behind them and moving in to ring us all, black men crowded through the doorways.

"For God's sake, cool it, Canby," Gilly shouted. "He's trouble, man."

Canby, the campus radical, and the other black man at the BMS meeting, had to be at least six-foot-six, and the height of the hair made him look much taller. He turned at Gilly's voice and bared his teeth in a nasty grin. "Trouble, Gillespie? That's trouble lying there. It isn't even good trouble. Good trouble is when you get something for your dying. All poor old Stanley Rhodes got was his comeuppance for doing business with the Man." He looked back to O'Malley. "That's called laying on the hands, Sheriff. It's a religious ceremony. Kind of like exorcism. Now I'm going to ask all you white folk to vacate the church. I understand sanctuary is an old white Anglo-Saxon custom. We're in sanctuary, us colored people."

O'Malley swept the ring of blacks with his eyes. For him or his men to draw guns was to precipitate a massacre. He straightened his topcoat and himself within it. "You make a mockery of religion, Canby. Just as you've tried to make a fool of me. And it won't work."

"A mockery of religion?" Canby raised his voice, a lost preacher among agnostics. "Oh, my people, what a mockery religion has made of you." Into the sheriff's face he said. "I'll be here until after the funeral, boss."

"You arrogant prick," the sheriff said, and shouldered his way through his own men who turned and followed him out of the church.

When they were gone, George Canby shrugged and looked at Gilly and me; at me with cold up-down insolence. He glanced back at Gilly and jerked his thumb toward the door. "The invitation out is universal. We don't need an obligatory white anymore, Gillespie. Go back where you came from, man, and no more brotherhood crap. It don't work, you know?"

He literally licked his lips to dramatize the special mockery he saved for me. Even in the presence of the dead, some of the men circling us laughed when he said, "White women make me rapist."

It was a long walk to the door. I did not want to, but my reporter's training bade me look back and absorb the last bitter dregs of the experience. But the black men now were moving in on the center of tragedy. Canby himself had turned away from us. He looked down at the lifeless figure and nodded in time with the women's moaning, a terrible rhythm of pain. His body began to twist jerkily and he kicked at the sprawled, stiffening feet. The last thing I saw was the doubling-over of that long, quivering body as he bent down and again covered the corpse. The men crowding in, blocked my view, but I had seen what I had to see to tell this story.

O'Malley was waiting for Gilly and me to come from the church. "I want the two of you to come into headquarters. I want your signed statement on what happened in there."

Gilly started to object.

"God damn it," O'Malley said, his eyes cold steel, "I could have required you to help me arrest him on the spot. This much cooperation you're going to give me, Gillespie . . ."

"Okay, okay," Gilly said. "They weren't so fucking glad to see me either."

We went back to Norah's car and drove out the way we had come in. By the time we reached Main Street, O'Malley was conferring at the barricade with the police chief, an ineffectual man named Bert Weber, and the black officers. Gilly explained to me about Weber and the municipal police: they had once been a legend of strength, built up by state law at the time of the great strike during the Depression. When the miners went back to work, the police force was reduced—ironically by the reemployment in the mines of some of the deputies whose police duty it had been to protect the scabs. Yet another amplification of that story first told me by Miss Ingrams.

We did not speak of the scene behind us at the church.

Gilly and I waited in the parking lot in back of the courthouse until the sheriff arrived. We followed him into the Operations Section. Which I had been ordered to leave a few ·hours before under pain of arrest for inciting to riot. There was not a man on duty that I recognized. I stayed on O'Malley's heels until he sat down at his desk without removing his topcoat.

"Something I want put straight on the record, Sheriff: Tarkington did *not* slap my face last night."

He just stared at me, through me. I was not even sure he heard me, and later I was sure he had not.

I heard one of the deputies who had come in with him instruct a desk officer to get him the "jacket" on George Canby. The file.

"Son of a bitch," the sheriff said under his breath, and a shudder ran through him. I have seen malaria affect people that way. Indeed, that passed through my mind because there was sweat on his forehead, and that youthful face looked haggard. Without a word to anyone, he got up from the desk and left.

The deputy waiting for the Canby file said, "Why don't you use the typewriter in the corner over there and do your own statements? Mrs. O'Malley was going to give us a hand, it being Saturday, but she's not showed up yet."

I did mine first, including a second page in which I set straight the sequence of incidents in the jail the night before. Then, because it's second nature to me to follow the news teletype where one is operating and I have nothing else to do, I read the police reports coming through while I waited for Gilly.

An armed robbery had occurred in Venice County during the night. There had been several breakings and entries, including a flower shop where only flowers had been stolen; there was a fire of questionable origin at Tate's Lumber Yard. I read with fascination that a white Impala Chevrolet had been stolen, license number . . .

Mrs. O'Malley came into the headquarters room.

I heard the deputy ask, "Where's the big man, Annie?"

"Taking a bath," she said.

The deputy gave a humorless laugh.

"Has there been any word on who . . . ?"

The question trailed off and I knew she had discovered Gilly and me. She came back slowly, the hostility unconcealed. She had on too much makeup. I thought it would not be so long until she would look like a tired whore. And O'Malley had that youthfulness about him that would be remarked on all his life.

She said to me, "You oughtn't to tell lies about the police, Mrs. Osborn It makes terrible trouble."

"I have said nothing about them, Mrs. O'Malley," and I gave her my account of the incident to read.

While she read it very carefully, she also carefully cleaned the lipstick from the corners of her mouth with her little finger. "That's better," she said, and gave me back the paper. "What are you going to do with it?"

"Sign it and leave it for the sheriff when he gets out of the bathtub."

Standing, I put my name to both statements, and left them with Gilly to turn over to the deputy. I waited for him outdoors.

From the county building Gilly and I drove to the Good Samaritan Hospital. The boys were sitting in the ward, dressed, waiting to be discharged. Yeager looked at Gilly as though he would rather not have seen him.

He said, "I blew it, didn't I, Gilly?"

"Somebody did."

"I'm sorry. I got carried away. You know . . ."

"Black Power," Gilly said. "It took over, didn't it?"

Yeager nodded sheepishly.

"When did you wake up to what was happening?"

"During breakfast—a couple of hours ago. The nurse brought in this big armful of flowers . . ." He nodded to where a large bouquet of yellow chrysanthemums and white carnations shared a vase on the table. "They'd been left downstairs with my name on them. I asked her who brought them. I mean, we didn't check in till midnight. Then when I read the card, I got this funny feeling of being made a fool of . . ." He dug the card from his pocket and handed it to Gilly. We both read the block letters: WITH THANKS FROM YOUR FRIENDS IN NIGGERTOWN

Yeager said, "Canby won't ever say Bakerstown, you know. It's always Niggerstown. All of a sudden I thought, they're all through with us. They don't give a shit for the BMS, they wanted a big stick to beat the white bosses with. I don't blame them . . . I guess. And I sure as hell don't love the coal mines, and my old man doesn't . . . But they're our thing, you know?"

"I know," Gilly said.

I wandered over and looked at the flowers. I was thinking of the breaking-and-entry report coming over the teletype at the sheriff's office: the stolen flowers.

"I feel awful, Gilly. We all do," Yeager said.

They all looked awful. Some of them wore patches, and one of them had his nose in a plaster. Both his eyes were blackened.

I had a couple of things I wanted to say to them, but first I asked, "Why wasn't Canby in jail with you, Mr. Yeager?"

"It was only the BMS members they picked up, ma'am. Now, wait a minute. I better fix that to read what I know for sure: what I think happened, I'm pretty sure they couldn't find him."

One of the other boys said, "That's shit, Alex; they didn't pick him up because they're afraid of the blacks' lawyers. These days you don't fuck around with those guys. You wait and get 'em on something you can make stick."

"That could be it, ma'am." Yeager turned to Gillespie. "Gilly, you don't think what happened at the jail last night—it couldn't've had anything to do with Rhodes' death, could it?"

"You tell us," Gilly said.

"I don't see how it could," Yeager said, but his voice was full of doubt.

Gilly and I were about to go.

Yeager blurted out: "I betrayed the Brotherhood, didn't I, Gilly?" And the big lump of a boy began to cry.

Gilly put a hand on his shoulder and shook him. "What you're forgetting, man, I'm the rotten informer that told the sheriff to look you up. May I keep this, Alex?" It was the card that had come with the flowers.

"Yeah. You can have the shitty flowers too."

"That's more like my boy," Gilly said, and clapped him on the back. "But for Christ's sake, stop talking for a while, will you?"

I had two observations to discuss with Gilly on the way back to the hotel. One was the makeup of the

146

flower bouquet: yellow chrysanthemums and white carnations don't mix. It seemed to me they were the indiscriminate loot from the burglary.

Gilly agreed.

"The other thing, Gilly—that card in your pocket —it says Niggertown, not Niggerstown."

"That's one of the reasons I wanted it," Gilly said. "And I wanted to make sure it didn't get lost. Whatever's to be said about George Canby, he's got taste. The flower business isn't his style at all. Which leaves the displaced deputies, doesn't it? 'Niggertown' is right on with their vocabulary."

Again I felt that faint annoyance with Gilly for the latter assumption in spite of the fact that nine chances out of ten he was right. I thought of Higgins and his tirade on right-wing bigots and opinionated left-wingers. Only fleetingly: more to the point was the sheriff taking a bath because a black man had laid his hands on him.

"What are you going to do with the card?"

"I ought to go to the police—if we're right about where the flowers came from. Only . . . I don't know, Kate, I'll poke around this morning. How are you going to get to The Hermitage? Do you want this heap?"

"Doesn't Forbes have a car?"

"I'd forgotten about him," Gilly said.

"Or should I arrange another rental?"

"Let's stop by there anyway," Gilly said.

✿ ✿ ✿

The rental agency had just opened, the manager himself the only one on hand. Saturday.

"Anything unusual happen around here last night?" Gilly asked.

"Compared to what's happening around, Gilly, not much. Got a stolen car report on one of our rentals."

"Mrs. Osborn's." Gilly said it like an introduction. "Now it looks as though the car was merely borrowed." He explained, meanwhile examining the board on which hung several sets of keys. "Duplicates?"

"Where there's two sets, the cars are in."

"The office wasn't broken into last night, was it?"

"I'm not sure it wasn't. But I'm not sure it was either." The manager explained that the lock on the door between the garage and the office wouldn't hold. It seemed to have been forced. "But the garage was locked up tight. Same with the front door."

Gilly thought for a moment. "Who does your servicing?"

"It's franchised to Macks' Chevrolet."

"So they'd have a garage key?"

"Sure."

"Anybody in particular you deal with over there?"

"Tarkington most of the time."

I arranged another rental. Unnecessarily, it turned out, but I had no way of knowing that at the time.

TWELVE

I got back to the Mardi Gras to find the whole staff in action. The reason: Steve Higgins was coming into town. I thought how fortunate I had not availed myself of the hospitality of his suite. He used it himself no oftener than once or twice a year. A message waiting me in my box: "Kate, I'm coming in at eleven this morning. Please be there. Steve."

I telephoned Forbes' home, and not getting him there, left the message with the physics department canceling that morning's engagement.

I have said the whole staff of the Mardi Gras was in action. Not so. Conspicuously absent were the black members. The housekeeper herself was making beds, and in the kitchen they had sent out a call for students, offering twice the minimum hourly wage. The blacks already on duty had walked out when word came of the shooting of the Reverend Rhodes. It was with this

149

facet of the tense situation in Venice that I commenced my feature material to *Saturday,* moving back through the occurrence in the Baptist Mission House to the discovery less than a day and a half before of the murdered body of the Nobel Laureate, Daniel Lowenthal. I phoned it in to Editorial. When I was through, Mike Fischer came on the phone.

"Didn't I tell you, Kate? A powder keg." And then presently: "Where's Higgins in all this?"

I said that he was moving into town in a half-hour.

Mike got excited. "You mean he's taking over?"

"I'm not sure, Mike. O'Malley's behaving very strangely. That whole family-jail setup is weird."

"Save the exotic for your own byline, Kate. I want a log on Big Steve every hour of the day. Stick with him. Go to bed with him if you have to. Power, Kate: if he's got it, he'll name the next President of the United States."

＊　＊　＊

Higgins arrived by limousine at ten minutes to eleven. He was accompanied by Laurie; by an adviser whom I had met at lunch at The Hermitage, Clint MacDowell, whose specialty was public relations, and, to my surprise, by Dingle, the gatekeeper who, when he saw me, grinned and patted beneath his arm so that I knew he had come along as a bodyguard. They were a curious spectacle, the four of them walking into the lobby. Higgins with his wide-brimmed hat and long, rancher's stride; Laurie, her notebook and pen in hand where she had been working all the way up from The Hermitage; Dingle, with his limp; and MacDowell, wearing a double-breasted suit. He put me in mind of a gangster's lawyer.

As soon as we got into the suite, Dingle and Mac-Dowell jacked in extra phones where Laurie said to put them.

Higgins said, "Kate, what's on the shortest fuse?"

"I'm inclined to say O'Malley. If he can't find a way out of the situation in Bakerstown, it's hard to say what he'd do."

"The first shot—is that what you mean?"

"It might happen. What am I talking about? It *has* happened."

"We had an agreement when he ran for sheriff last time: he wasn't to make a move in Bakerstown without a man named Percy Anderson. See if he's come yet, Laurie."

Anderson was a state senator, black and beholden, Higgins said. He had just come into the lobby when Laurie phoned down. While he was on his way upstairs I gave Higgins my version of the scene at the Baptist Mission. I stopped short of telling him Canby's reference to me. By then O'Malley had been outside the church, or so I had thought. It did not seem necessary to repeat that bit of abuse.

Higgins brought his fist down on the table with such force that the phone jumped out of its cradle. I also jumped. "Don't censor, Kate! This is no time for mush."

"Okay, Steve." I did not again try to withhold anything from him. I told him of the circumstances and the "theft" of my rented car and the ease with which Tarkington might have got hold of the keys. "I'm not accusing him, but it's a lot of coincidence."

"He's an inferior whelp," Higgins said with contempt. He turned to MacDowell. "Clint, get the names of the deputies suspended last night. I mean the men actually present when O'Malley read them out of action. Do it this way: get hold of Everett and play it light, confidential. One of the things we're going to have to figure out is who outside this room—if anybody —we can trust."

When the doorbell rang Steve signaled to Dingle. Dingle had already assumed the role of sergeant-at-arms.

"I have one candidate, Steve," I said. "Hold onto your hat: Andrew Gillespie."

Higgins grinned. "On the contrary, Kate. After what those kids did to him and his organization last night, I'd trust him to the Kremlin and back. Tell Laurie how to get hold of him." He was on his feet, his hand outstretched across the table, when the black man came into the room ahead of Dingle.

I wanted to reach Gilly fast. When Laurie got Norah on the phone I asked Norah to track him down which, considering that it meant riding his bicycle into town, was a large favor. I also asked her not to go home again before calling me from the lobby of the Mardi Gras. It seemed to me there was a place for her in this contingency setup.

Steve introduced me to Percy Anderson, an athletic-looking man with a quick, useful smile. He wore a business suit, but a turtleneck sweater and a peace pendant on a leather thong.

"Have you been over there yet?" Higgins asked him.

"No. I want to make sure how I go in. I might not

get a second chance if I blew it the first time. I talked to a couple of people, talked to Ida Rhodes' brother, in fact. She heard the shot, got up and called down to Stan if he was all right, and somebody answered her, 'I'm all right.' So she figured it was a backfire on Route 32 and went back to bed till she heard the car speed away. Anyway . . ."

"Tell it all," Steve said. "This isn't the way I got it and I want it straight."

"Well, she lay in bed and thought about it. It was getting more and more daylight . . ."

"What was he doing out at that hour?"

"Getting the feel of morning. There was going to be a sunrise service come Easter, and not being able to sleep, he decided to give himself a dress rehearsal."

"He was shot at close range?" Steve asked.

"Pretty close. You see, he'd caught whoever it was who shot him in the act of tying rags or sheets around that iron cross outside the Mission. They were going to have themselves a flash cross-burning."

"So he'd 've recognized them."

"Could be, Steve."

I thought of the sheets covering the body of Rhodes inside the church.

"It sounds like something you'd do on a drunken spree," Higgins said. "I mean the cross part. Anybody sober would start with a wooden cross."

"I'm no authority," Anderson said. The teeth flashed, and that time there was ice in the smile.

"The way I heard it, it was a milk driver found the body," Higgins said.

"You could say that, but it went more like this: Ida found the parson, and the milk driver found Ida.

She'd just started to scream. She went downstairs and out to the church when she couldn't go back to sleep and didn't hear anything and then the parson didn't come back to bed. It was the driver all right who put in the call to the police."

"How do you stand on George Canby, Percy?"

"I'm going to tell you the truth, Steve. I admire the kid. He's smart and he's cool."

"Does he know you feel that way about him?"

"Steve, with these cats I'm just a half-inch taller than Parson Rhodes, and by them he was an Uncle Tom. They don't give a damn how I feel."

"How does this idea strike you: we'll fly in a black undertaker from Saint Louis, say, use the black municipal police, and do the autopsy right there in the church?"

"That might do fine in Bakerstown but how do you think they'll take it in the rest of Venice? O'Malley's a mighty popular man."

"Let me worry about O'Malley and his image."

"Forgive me, chief," the black man said, "but it isn't you the white citizens are going to take it out on."

"Get the message over there, Percy, and let's see what happens."

Higgins watched him to the door. When he got there Higgins said, "If they come up with a compromise that would get us into action faster, I'd like to hear about it."

Anderson gave a wry smile of understanding.

I said, "Steve, it's important that nothing happens to those sheets. They could lead somewhere."

"Hear that, Percy?"

"I heard."

It was like watching a dervish in action: behind the big table Higgins sat in a marvelously mobile posture chair, and more than once I thought that he rode it with a mastery that came of horsemanship. As soon as Anderson left he was on the phone with the editor of the *Downstate Independent*. He had him read the story on Rhodes' killing and the present situation in Bakerstown.

"Get this paragraph in where it belongs and then lock up. Ready? 'With State Senator Percy Anderson as arbiter, Sheriff John J. O'Malley agreed late this morning to an on-the-scene autopsy by the county medical examiner. It is expected that the findings will greatly hasten the arrest, and so forth . . .'

"Now, that BMS story, or whatever the hell they call it, the university kids from the mines? Kill it. Instead, let's have something along these lines: Hold it a minute . . . Laurie take this down because you're going to have to get through to both mine bosses before the paper hits the town. Okay, here we go: 'Steve Higgins, principal shareholder in Red Devil Mines One and Two, announced a new on-the-job training program late yesterday afternoon. It will be set up under an advisory council headed by Hugh Bourke, dean and so forth . . . Meanwhile, according to Mr. Higgins, no Vietnam veteran applying for work in the mines will be turned down by management. The extent to which the mine workers' union will cooperate remains to be worked out.' Thirty. And put it where people are going to read it.

"Let's run the jail story as it is, because it's important that we support O'Malley in his suspension of the Blue Hats . . ." The editor obviously shocked him with new information. His face flushed, he hung up in that abrupt, no-explanation way of his, and roared out to MacDowell in the other room, "Clint! For Christ Jesus' sake, what are you doing in there? O'Malley has called them all back into service."

MacDowell opened the door. He had carried the phone with him, and mouthed to Steve that it was O'Malley himself on the line. He kept mumbling "Yes, that's right," and so on. Finally he said, "I'll pass the word on to Steve, John J. I think he'd like it if you took him into your confidence on the next move . . ."

Steve hardly waited for the click of the phone. "I don't like being double-crossed, especially by John Joseph."

"In a way he makes sense, Steve. Mrs. Osborn signed a statement this morning saying it wasn't so that she'd been pushed around by the deputies, so he felt the best thing he could do to make up to them was revoke the suspension."

I said, "But they weren't suspended on account of me. It was for what they did to the boys, wasn't it?"

Higgins massaged the back of his neck. "Kate, you got to stop apologizing. It doesn't do any good in a situation like this. It's like trying to blow out a fire that's getting bigger all the time. Most people in this town would say the boys had it coming to them—making peepee all over Mrs. O'Malley's hash—but striking a lady—that's a terrible thing. What else did he say, Clint?"

"That Judge Doight just issued a warrant for the arrest of George Canby, and that O'Malley was going to personally execute it if it was the last thing he ever did."

"Isn't that splendid and courageous of him! What a time for a personal vendetta."

"He's got a real thing against the blacks, hasn't he?" I said. "Why?"

"Because he grew up fighting them for jobs, that's why. And someplace deep down in there he isn't sure he won out for the right reasons. That's his whole trouble; he's not sure he got anything because he deserved it. He hates gifts, but he takes them all the same. He's afraid that if he doesn't, he'll offend the donor. He wants to make it on his own, but he's afraid if he does that he'll make enemies. He's afraid, period. Only one thing makes him brave—hatred. And that's because it blinds him first."

I thought of Mrs. O'Malley reading my statement on the jail incident. I wondered aloud if she was behind the reinstatement of the Blue Hats.

"Possible. But she'd make him think it was his idea."

"I'd have thought he was cleverer than her," I said.

"Then you'd be wrong," he snapped.

       ✿   ✿   ✿

Gilly called me from the lobby. He had not known that I was trying to find him; he had something important to tell me, but not on the phone.

"Tell him to come up," Higgins said. "I'll leave the room for five minutes."

Gilly came, his beard bristling ahead of him. He was both in awe and very leery of Higgins. Higgins got up and came around the table. He shook hands, saying,

"I knew your father and, if I'm not mistaken, your grandfather."

I explained to Gilly why we were trying to get hold of him.

"You understand, young man, this does not commit you to capitalism," Higgins said, a twinkle in his eye.

Gilly merely blinked his eyes, waiting, impervious to blandishment. He said, when Steve and I stopped the unnecessary persuasion, "I went back over some old ground, Kate, and broke some that's new, and I've put a couple of things together. The flowers that were stolen during the night were mums and carnations, yellow and white. I found a beat-up yellow mum on the floor of your car."

I felt a knot in my stomach, for now I was sure that every madness of the night was connected. I said, "Gilly, tell it the way you think it goes."

Higgins went back to his chair and signaled Laurie, whom he introduced to Gilly also as plain Laurie, to get what Gillespie had to say in her notebook.

"The time is approximate," Gilly started. "Eleven to twelve, BMS boys released from county jail. They proceed on their own to Good Samaritan Hospital. Taxi and M.D. give them rides. First to hear story of beatings. M.D. and hospital resident look them over: patches, stitches, general repairs, and M.D. advises resident to hold them overnight for observation. With successful hospitalization following the jail beating, the kids figure it's great stuff for publicity. Yeager gets carried away with his own importance. Phones Canby. Canby tells him what he ought to say to the press.

Yeager calls press conference. Big shot. Continues to avoid senior officer of the Brotherhood—me. Maybe four reporters show up, most of them lodgers at the Mardi Gras, on hand to cover investigation of murder of Daniel Lowenthal, Nobel Laureate, distinguished citizen of world. What investigation?

"Hungry reporters eat up the story of police-student confrontation in jail. Any violence is better than none. Story filed in St. Louis and Chicago papers. Even covered by *Downstate Independent* and mobile radio unit.

"Meanwhile, back in the sheriff's office, the Blue Hats were suspended, pending investigation of boys' brutality charges . . ." Gilly looked Higgins straight in the eyes. "Once more, O'Malley's special police are curbed by the persuasion of downstate Democratic boss, Steve Higgins. Which will win Higgins the approval of the so-called liberal community. The campus, in other words. The majority, silent and not so silent, will sympathize with O'Malley and his men. In the normal course of events, they would soon go back into uniform.

"But things in Venice are far from normal. The elite corps of the Blue Hats, unfrocked by O'Malley and Higgins, find a bar, a regular hangout maybe. For reasons I'll come to soon, I suspect it's on County Road which used to be called Roadhouse Lane, which takes them past my house, coming and going. I'd guess that some of them dropped out early, maybe in the beginning. But maybe two or three by then—I don't know— get drunker and meaner. They sit around licking their wounds. Somebody turns on the news to see if they made it, and, man, did they make it! Not only are they accused of beating up the kids, but one of them is falsely charged with taking a poke at a lady. These knights in shining armor. And the dirty kids are out free, spouting Red socialism and black supremacy, you might say. The rest isn't very funny, so I'm going to do it straight."

"For God's sake, do," Higgins said without cracking a smile, "before I die laughing."

"I don't know the order in which these things happened," Gilly went on, "but I'm pretty sure they happened. I've got a famous local address, Mr. Higgins, a former speakeasy . . ."

"I knew it before you were born," Higgins said.

"Right. They would have spotted Kate's car outside my place and one of them, Tarkington, might have recognized it right off. He services most of the rentals. Anyway, somewhere in there, coming or going, he picked up the duplicate set of keys at the shop and they borrowed Kate's car. They broke into Metzger's Flower Shop and helped themselves to a mixed bouquet which they delivered to the hospital for the boys —a big joke. Here's the message." He handed Steve the card. Steve laid it on the table and stared at it while Gilly went on.

"I'm not sure what else they were into, or how many of them were involved. That's police work—if there are police around who can be trusted to do it. And I'll say this, because I've been thinking about it: I don't think now they meant Kate any great harm. They were out to give her a scare. But they were drunk, I think, and the mischief they got into kept snowballing.

I'm on shaky grounds with the rest of this: there was a fire this morning at Post's Lumber Yard, and the smell of gasoline is very strong inside Kate's car, as though some had been spilled there . . ."

I had not realized that I had clenched my fist until Higgins reached over and patted it.

"I don't think they had anything to do with the fire," he said, "but you're close to the nail up till then. Let's see if I can do as good a job with the rest of the story. Whoever killed Parson Rhodes . . . No. Let's put it this way: at dawn the parson left his bed and went outdoors, intending to go into the Mission House. He surprised somebody getting ready to wrap bedsheets— which could have been stolen from the hospital; that's a distinct possibility—around the cross in the front yard. They were going to pour gasoline on the sheets and set fire to them, but when the parson saw them, recognized them, one of them drew his service revolver and shot him. After that it was a matter of getting rid of the car as soon as possible and getting home."

"But what a risk," I said, "to park it in the hotel lot; the chance of being seen by a hotel employee."

"They also took the keys back to the rental agency," Gilly said.

"There may have been some cover we don't know about," Higgins said, "and some more carelessness they don't know about. Like the stray chrysanthemum." He carefully lifted the card, WITH THANKS FROM YOUR FRIENDS IN NIGGERTOWN, and put it in an envelope. "Exhibit number one for the grand jury. Laurie, get John Joseph on the phone for me."

"Why do you call him John Joseph?" I asked.

"Because his mother-in-law called him that." But on the phone he asked for O'Malley. And to him: "John . . . I'm here, you know, if you need me . . ."

That was the beginning of one of the most remarkable telephone conversations I have ever listened in on. Higgins thrust a finger at me to indicate I was to take the extension phone from Laurie. There was a private line into the suite, accounting for the complexities of phone usage. I'm not going to be able to do justice to that conversation because a very large part of its success depended on vocal nuance. Nevertheless:

"Clint tells me you've got a bench warrant for the arrest of Canby. It's time that black boy got his come-uppance. But what about your boys, John J.? Is it true you called them back to duty?"

O'Malley: "I may need them, Steve. If that happens, I didn't want to have to crawl on my belly. This way I've still got authority."

"I see. I didn't think you'd be congratulating them on beating up the kids."

"They didn't beat up any kids, Steve. Everybody was swinging in there; some of my boys got hurt too, but they didn't run crying to the hospital. That was for the press. You got to remember where that Osborn woman comes from, Steve. That's publicity country. When she went down to the bullpen to see those kids last night—as Tarkie says, they should've known right then that something would blow up before the night was out."

"Tarkie says that, does he?" But said absolutely straight. "Has he signed in this morning?"

"He's here."

"What's his business in civilian life, John J.?"

"He's a mechanic up at the Chevrolet shop."

"Ah, yes. Within earshot now?"

"He's got his ears up."

"But that's all," somebody said, close enough to the phone to be heard. As was the general laughter also.

"John J., did everybody come back? No hard feelings?"

"They're here. I don't know what their feelings are yet. They've got a job to do if Bakerstown blows its lid."

"What's your strategy?"

"Ring it round and move in slow."

"What about serving that warrant?"

"I'm going to have to play it by ear, Steve. What I figure now, I'll bullhorn in to them to send him out. The same with Rhodes' body . . ."

"By God, I'd almost forgotten," Higgins said. His eyes flashed steel, but the voice had a silken purr.

"The way we've set it up here, give them a couple of hours. A corpse needs taking care of. I figure living with it will bring them to their senses. I don't want to start off any shooting match. Only if we have to, we're going to be ready this time."

Higgins said, "Percy Anderson was trying to get through to you, John J. He's got a black undertaker coming in, and he thought you might be willing to have the autopsy done right there in Bakerstown."

"That might work out—if I get Canby first."

"I don't suppose you've got very far in tracking down Rhodes' killer?"

"Steve, how can you investigate a murder if you don't have the corpse?"

Higgins made a noise that might have been agreement. "What I'm going to do, John J., I'm coming over to headquarters, and I'll bring Mrs. Osborn with me. Maybe she could help straighten things out with the boys herself." He did not look at me.

"Hell, Steve, that's not necessary. She gave her affidavit when she was here earlier this morning."

"Face to face is better," Steve cajoled.

"Yeah, but she's got two faces and the boys don't know which one to look at."

That, I admit, shook me badly. There was no reason for him to say it if he did not believe it, if it were not the consensus of his men. God-damn Tarkington.

"A half hour or so," Higgins said, and hung up the phone. He swung around to me. "How does that make you feel, Mrs. Osborn?"

I shook my head and said to Gilly, "He called me two-faced."

Gilly said, "Beauty is in the eyes of the beholder."

I thought of Lowenthal and supposed that Gilly might have also. But Higgins surprised me, saying to Gilly: "Had you any idea about Professor Lowenthal going to East Germany?"

"No, sir, but I don't find it all that terrible."

"Then why was it such a secret?"

"That's a good question, Mr. Higgins."

"Thank you," Steve said dryly. "I know some good answers too . . . Laurie, what time did Anderson leave here?"

"It's over an hour, Steve."

"I wonder what the hell's going on over there. A ten-minute drive."

"A couple of reporters went with him," Gilly said.

"I don't know why they turned on me in Bakerstown this morning, but they did."

"You're white," I said. "That's all there is to it, Gilly. Obligatory white: Canby said it."

Steve said, "If there's a confrontation like I believe the sheriff in his heart is praying for—which side will you be on, Gillespie?"

After a moment: "White, whether I wanted to or not."

"So it isn't very complicated after all—only in your conscience."

"I guess," Gilly said.

"Steve, I don't want to go back to the sheriff's office. I don't ever want to go back there, really."

"I said that to gain us time—hoping to keep the army in their barracks."

MacDowell came from the other room. "Here's your black undertaker, Steve." He handed him a piece of paper on which the name was written. "I got him from Springfield. I thought you'd like that better than St. Louis: support for home industries. He's on his way."

Higgins sat, his elbows on the desk, his chin in his hands. "I ought to call the governor," he said, "but Lord God Almighty, I hate to do that."

"In case you need the National Guard?"

"That's why I'd call him," Steve said, "but the reasons not to call him go a little deeper. That's one favor a politician doesn't like asked of him, Kate. You're damned if you call the Guard out and you're damned if you don't. And no matter how beholden the governor might be to me, it's his head that wears the crown. I don't want to ask him to put it on the block."

I remembered and said: "When O'Malley was trying to get Rhodes' body, he threatened to bring in the National Guard."

"They're easier to threaten with than the Blue Hats," Higgins said. "And safer. For one thing, they have to be mobilized and that takes longer."

"And at that point I don't think he intended to reinstate the Blue Hats right away," I said.

"He went into the ghetto without them," Gilly said.

I went on: "Which brings us back to what you and I said earlier: that the idea to reinstate them might have come from *Mrs.* O'Malley."

Higgins' eyes snapped. "You don't like her much, do you, Kate?"

Laurie gave a Ha! that made him grin.

The phone rang. Higgins took it himself. It was Norah for me. I explained to Steve and he said to have her sent up. He began to pace, which did not help our nerves any. When Norah arrived he suspended his worry long enough to look her over. From long hair to high boots. "So *you're* Norah," he said.

"You've forgotten. I work for you, Mr. Higgins." Norah flashed him a smile.

"I've never known a man with better taste," he said.

He stood then, leaning his hands on his desk. He stared at the envelope in which he had put the card accompanying the flowers. "Kate, you and I are going out to lunch. The rest of you can hold down here. We'll check in periodically. Get some food sent up, Laurie, unpack the booze, and settle in. It may be a long siege. Dingie, bring the car round front." To me again: "Do you want to . . . ?" He shook his hand out, a spinning motion.

"Yes, I want to. I'll meet you in the lobby in five minutes."

Gilly was grinning like a child who had crawled under the circus tent and wound up in a box seat. That was one of the things you learned about Steve Higgins: he could make you forget how really grim a job was at hand.

He was waiting at the bottom of the stairs and took my arm. The bellboy sprinted to open the door, Steve all but carrying me through the lobby with him.

As we got into the car, Steve said, "We're giving that young fellow up there a lesson in democracy, eh, Kate? Democracy at work."

THIRTEEN

The car was a Lincoln Continental. The glass was tinted so that you could see out easily enough, but it was almost impossible to see in. Dingle, in a pea jacket and crumpled cap, looked completely out of place. Behind the wheel of a battered cab, yes, but as chauffeur for that luxury liner, no. More democracy, I thought.

"Roadhouse Lane," Steve directed. "Stop first at Minnie Moran's."

I set myself to watching for Gilly's house while Steve got the phone operating. He checked in with Laurie just to make sure his communications lines were straight. I thought of Kovac in my hotel room and Forbes yanking the bug in the jail bullpen. I said, half-joking, "Aren't you afraid there's a tap on the phone, Steve?"

"I know how to jam the signal."

I was surprised. "Do you accept the possibility of wiretap that casually?"

"Kate, don't you realize that privacy today is an anachronism? Look around you. The sex scene, for example: groups. Look at international diplomacy. No more secrecy: you do things now by distraction. A scandal in the Pentagon, say, and meanwhile you can be shaking hands with Fu Manchu or whoever the hell. Look at the movies: what's left out? Nothing. Every time they bleep the television, it's laughable. A kid sitting playing with himself in front of the set fills in all the words. That's what they call growing up natural. I don't know if it's good and I don't know if it's bad. I don't know what the hell it is, Kate. I just know it's the way it is, and since I want to live till I die, I'm playing it back the way it comes at me. Ask me what you want to know and I'll tell you. I'll save you wasting time digging through the gossip."

"Time for what? There has to be some discovery, some mystery to life, Steve."

"Well, you just think about all the lights they keep burning all night long in Venice, and then look at the dark things happening. When you can see everything, after a while who looks?"

"There's Gilly's house," I said, "coming up at the top of the rise." We were passing the trailer camp.

He turned and stared back, counting the trailers. "My God, they'll all be eligible to vote under the new law. We'd better see that they're registered." He twisted restlessly in the car seat. I realized what it meant.

"Steve, do you want me to make a note and give it to Laurie?"

He laughed and put his hand on mine where it lay ungloved in my lap. A real shock came to me with the erotic response I felt at his touch.

"In the midst of death there is life," he said, so that I supposed the current ran both ways. He squeezed my hand and released it; then putting his arm on the plush upholstery behind me, he gently prisoned my head and kissed me, his tongue stroking my lips until he had parted them. He tasted of hickory, an outdoors taste.

"Coming up on Minnie's, Steve," Dingle said.

Higgins sat back and chortled softly.

That was a mistake, Katherine, I said to myself: or was it? I suspected sex to be one more symbol of power to him, and I wondered if he would trust a woman who didn't want to go to bed with him. There was something blatantly open about him.

          ❋   ❋   ❋

We drove up to a restaurant called the Shamrock Inn: long ago it had lost whatever charm it might once have had. The paint was peeling. The remnants of window boxes hung broken and empty except where one was strong enough to serve as a waste basket. The smell of grease saturated the air, and Steve said, "You're in the land of chicken-fried steak, Kate. Does it turn your stomach?"

"Not at the moment."

Dingle was left to monitor the phone while we went in the side door. Two men were having steak sandwiches and beer at the bar, watching a Felix the Cat cartoon on television. Higgins beckoned to the barman and ordered Old Granddad.

170

"Where's Minnie?"

"Lying down. Saturdays is slow till suppertime."

"Get her up," Steve said. "Tell her an old friend wants to see her."

The barman did not ask his name. Maybe he knew it. In any case, there was in Steve's way of saying "old friend" an authority that forbade you to doubt it. We took our bourbon to a table beside a window: from it we could see the car. Steve signaled Dingle with his handkerchief. Dingle lowered the window so we could see him salute, and then raised it again. It had remained a cold, gray day.

"You know, that car's got everything but indoor plumbing," Steve said.

"Just like Bakerstown," I said.

"Aw, Kate, stop hanging around with that fella, Gillespie. But doesn't he have a beautiful girl? Norah what? She's Irish, isn't she?"

"Fallon," I said. "Irish to the core."

"Probably frigid."

"I doubt it," I said with a degree of briskness.

He grinned.

"God save the Holy Ghost!" The cry came at us in a husky female voice.

Higgins rose to his feet and I looked up to see a Tugboat Annie of a woman, large, hearty, and floppy.

"My God, Min," Higgins said, and the brogue crawled into his voice, "you're fading away to a ton."

"Steve! You're as bony-assed as ever."

"Meet Kate Osborn." To me he explained, "Minnie is one of the last of the riverboat entertainers, and she can still belt out a song."

"Listen to me," she said and made a hoarse moan.

"I belted out a few last night, and I belted in a few. I can't drink the way I used to. Sit down, man, that's what the chairs are for. Ah, Steve—there's nothing takes the place of youth. Memory is a dry whistle. How's Dingle?"

"He's out in the car. I'll send him in to say hello after a while. Can I buy you a drink, Minnie—the hair of the dog?"

She ignored the invitation and screwed up her eyes as she asked, "What are you here for? Don't say it's my cooking, for you've not et a meal here since they restored my license. Is it to do with . . . the black man?"

"I wouldn't say that, Minnie."

"I know you wouldn't say it; that's why I'm asking."

"The answer is no . . . I'd forgotten about that licensing business . . ."

"The hell you did. If there was ever anything we had in common it was speaking our minds. You don't have to start beating around the bush now."

He nodded. "Sit down, Minnie, and have a drink for old times' sake."

She pulled up a chair and while she didn't straddle it, she rode it sidesaddle, her arm on the back so that she looked at Higgins over it—and exposed to me, beneath the dress that climbed higher and higher, the lumpy fallout of flesh that her skin could not hold in any longer. She jerked her head in my direction. "Is this the one that started it all?"

So, I thought, this is where the displaced deputies put in. Gilly knew what he was talking about.

"That's one way of putting it," Higgins said. "She

was only doing her job—which she does uncommonly well. Have you got a picture of yourself around from the old days, Minnie? Kate's a real newspaper woman. She's doing what they call a profile of me, and I've already told her about life along the river when I was laying up a fortune—among other things."

"A dry whistle," she repeated and made a disparaging little sound from behind her false teeth. She did not even play the game to the extent of admitting she had pictures. I had already seen one myself over the bar. Both she and I knew I didn't want her picture. "Who are you looking for, Steve? You must want him awful bad to come out of The Hermitage."

"Who was here when you turned on the news?"

"How did you know we turned on the news?"

"I guessed it."

"Then guess who was here. I'm not a bloody informer, Steve. They work damn hard to make that town a safe place to live in . . ."

He cut in: "O'Malley called them back to work this morning, Minnie."

"Then he must've had desperate need of them."

"How many were here?"

"Five . . . six, including—everybody."

"Whose car?"

"A sheriff's."

Their eyes met in a combat I did not understand.

"Spill it all, Minnie."

Nothing.

"Sweetheart?"

"You're such a lovable bastard, Steve." She got up and pushed the chair under the table and then waddled to the bar. She moved sidewise past the bartender and reached up to take what I supposed was a picture from the apron overhead. I could not see what it was until she brought it back and handed it to Higgins. "I was going to retire soon anyway, Steve. Maybe you ought to do the same thing. We're both getting out of tune, and there's not a license in the world that'll fix that."

What she put in his hands was the permit of the Shamrock Inn.

"The drinks are on the house," she said to the bartender as she disappeared through the curtained doorway.

Steve sat back, grinning. To me he said, holding his shot glass between two fingers, "Makes you feel good about your own generation, guts like that." He downed the drink, as I did mine, and he left two dollars under the framed license.

Dingle got out and opened the car door for us. "How's Minnie?"

"She sends you her love . . . she's just fine. Nothing yet?"

"No word. It says on the radio they're putting up barricades all around Bakerstown, blockading themselves in."

"I like that, Dingie—blockading themselves in. Did they really say that on the radio?"

His mood had changed: I couldn't quite judge it, no more than I knew what had really passed between him and the Moran woman. It was a grimmer mood; the self-confidence more measured . . . A little mockery had set in. That was it: self-mockery, which would also allow him to gently mock Dingle whom he considered an extension of himself.

"You're not hungry, are you, Kate?"

"I can wait." I was having trouble remembering when I had eaten. At Gilly's before the news came on. I knew I had not yet had breakfast and it was one in the afternoon.

"Turn back into town, Dingie."

On the way back we stopped and I pointed out where I'd left the car while I was in Gilly's. There was a road sign advertising the Mardi Gras Inn a few yards on. Higgins said it was often used as a cover for police cars to trap the speeders.

We drove on. Steve took a gold flask from his inside pocket and sat silent with it in his hand for a mile or so. Then, as he unscrewed the cap, he leaned forward. "Dingie, turn right at the next corner and let's go in town on Route 32."

"Through Bakerstown?"

"That's what I have in mind."

FOURTEEN

Higgins made me repeat what had happened to both Gilly and me and to O'Malley in the Mission House that morning. He seemed to be memorizing the scene.

"Obligatory white," he mumbled. "Obligatory to whom, eh? Isn't that the question?"

And on what happened to O'Malley: "Canby actually laid hands on him, did he?"

"He lifted him from the ground, one hand between his buttocks."

"Bad, bad," he said, shaking his head. He sipped from the flask and handed it to me.

"The whole purpose was to hurt back in every way he could," I said.

It was the golden bourbon, but on an empty stomach it plummeted like mercury.

"He sure got O'Malley in a vulnerable spot."

I thought of Forbes and the students' comment on his vulnerability in the same area. I'm inclined to discount young men's appraisal of the sexuality of their elders, which, at the moment, was neither here nor there. I said, "Steve, why did you want me to bring Forbes out with me today?"

"To have a look at the man myself. I wanted to see how he would take the news of Lowenthal going to East Germany."

"You knew it last night—when I called you?"

"We had just wound up a meeting with the FBI. We didn't know the Germans would blow the story ahead of us."

I thought about the scene at The Hermitage: the secret kind of conclave, and I asked bluntly: "Why at The Hermitage?"

He grunted at my abruptness and didn't answer until he had taken back the flask from me and put it away in his pocket. "Why, because Hugh Bourke and other university people were also present."

"But not Forbes. He wasn't invited."

"Not Forbes. He's in a highly ambiguous position."

"He's a highly ambiguous man," I said. "He would like me to believe the police suspect him of Lowenthal's murder."

"They do. Has it occurred to you, Kate, that that might be what he was trying to find out from you, the extent to which he is suspected?"

I laughed dryly. "He's certainly going about it in a devious manner then . . . I thought he was trying to tell me he was falling in love with me."

"That would be a useful message to get across," Higgins said.

I shot him a sidewise glance.

"Sorry, Kate. Won't I do?" It was said in mock seriousness.

"For at least ten," I said.

Dingle said over his shoulder, "There's a police block ahead, Steve."

"Sheriff or municipal?"

"I don't see any Blue Hats." A moment later: "Sheriff's regulars and the municipals."

Steve sat forward, and the moment the limousine came to a halt he got out and spoke with the officer in command. He got back into the car. The barricade was removed and he told Dingle to drive on to the Democratic Club.

Every street was piled with trash at the place where it intersected Route 32. Old mattresses were of as high priority here as they were on the Lower East Side of New York. I thought of Forbes again: *Don't you think we're civilized?*—This of the torn-out telephone.

"You know an observation I think it's worthwhile making, Kate? They're making all sorts of preparations in the town against vandalism, and these people are getting ready to burn *themselves* down."

"It does look like that," I murmured.

Dingle's neck was as stiff as concrete. I wondered if the appearance of such a limousine as Higgins' crawling along the perimeter of the ghetto might not trigger the very action he hoped to forestall. We passed a number of youngsters piling up ammunition: rocks and bottles, cans . . . I saw youths piping gasoline out of car tanks into bottles . . . I saw an assembly line for making slingshots: two boys cutting up tire tubes, two others fixing the strips to forked sticks. But not a stick or a stone was sailed our way. People simply stopped and stared. As in a picket line, twenty or so men and women walked back and forth in front of the Mission House.

"So far, so good," Dingle said, pulling up in front of the new brick building with the banner hanging from its two second-floor windows proclaiming it to be the Democratic Club. There were not many such buildings in Bakerstown.

"Don't say it," Higgins said, reading my mind. "It's even got shower baths and toilets."

I caught sight of a sign over a side door. "And a drug clinic."

"Yes. We're *au courant,* as the French would say."

Anderson was on the phone with Laurie when we got inside. He was in his shirtsleeves, but sweating nonetheless. My friend, Stu Rosen, was one of the two reporters with him.

Higgins said, "Tell her Kate and I are here and hang up." And when Anderson got off the phone: "What are you doing in here instead of out there where the action is?"

This time Anderson did not smile. His lips curled down and he wiped the sweat from his face on his shirtsleeve. "Get yourself another nigger, Steve. You can't talk to me that way."

"Which means you've failed, doesn't it? They want no part of the proposition. How long since you've made contact with them at the church?"

"A half-hour ago."

"Any split in the ranks?"

Anderson shook his head. "Canby's got them in the palm of his hand. Everything or nothing."

For the first time Steve's eyes rested on Rosen, then on the other man. He was looking for signs of agreement or disagreement with Anderson's opinion.

"What's everything?" he snapped.

"Burn, baby, burn. A funeral pyre."

"That's *nothing!*" Steve gave one of his mighty thumps on the table. "I want to know what's *everything*."

"The killer of Parson Rhodes with a rope around his neck."

"That's more like it," Steve said. "Where's Canby now?"

"In Ida's house. Or in the church."

"He doesn't live in the ghetto, does he?"

"International House on campus."

"Still there? Funny I'd forget that after last year, isn't it?" Steve was reshaping the crown of his hat.

I had found a half-can of stale peanuts from which I ate steadily.

"I don't live here either," Anderson said.

"And funnier still *he*'d forget it," Steve said with the snap of a steel trap. "We'll drive you to the church, Percy. Then I want you to send Canby out to the car to me."

"Man, I couldn't send Canby to the shithouse if he had diarrhea."

"Put your coat on and let's see." He shook hands with the reporters then. "Why don't you fellows go on ahead to the church? That's where it's going to happen."

"Do you want another opinion, Mr. Higgins?" Stu said.

"Till I'm in the grave."

"If it wasn't for Canby, I think he could swing them." He nodded at Anderson.

"You know, my friend, I think so too."

When there were only the two of us in the room, Higgins picked up the phone, dialed a number and waited. He winked at me. I thought of a gambler waiting the throw of the dice. I heard the singsong answer of a woman's voice.

Then Higgins: "Hello, Annie, what are you doing on the switchboard?" A complete change of pace: Southern leisureliness. "Saturday . . . That's right, I'd forgotten. I'd like to speak to John Joseph . . ."

Annie said something. Higgins' eyes narrowed but the voice remained honeyed. "Every available man, I suppose? . . . They'll be stopping at the armory first, won't they?" He nodded, getting an affirmative answer.

"Annie, you were a very bad girl last night. If I were you, I'd just let that switchboard go and try and catch up with John Joseph and tell him about it."

I don't know how she responded except that it had to be a denial.

"Okay, baby, we'll just have to wait and see whose funeral is next." This time he cradled the phone very gently.

On his way out he put his arm across the shoulders of the state senator. "Percy, you'd be surprised how little time we've got left in this town, and how few options. I want you to say to Canby . . . Let's see, what *do* I want you to say to him? Say this to him: 'Let the dead bury the dead.' If he's half the revolutionary he thinks he is, that's going to get through to him. Tell him I said it: 'Let the dead bury the dead,' and bring him out to see me in the car."

When we left the building Anderson carried a bundle, which he put on the floor in front of us on Steve's order: two sheets bearing the stamp of the Good Samaritan Hospital.

Again Dingle drove with an almost insidious slowness. We approached Stu and the other reporter who broke into a jog when we came nearer.

"Stop the car," Steve ordered. "Open the window."

Dingle pushed a button. The dashboard was a veritable pipe organ of controls.

Steve said to the reporters, "*Walk,* gentlemen, please don't run. We don't want any unnecessary alarms."

The window closed and we moved on. They watched us come from in front of the Mission House, the pickets slowing down into a cluster. Within the last few yards, Steve said, "Percy, it's in your hands now. Make it work, man. It's the chance of a lifetime, I promise you."

We stopped at the curb where a man was taking down the cross, length by length of pipe. Anderson left the car door open behind him at Steve's order, and moved up the walk. The people alongside made desultory responses to whatever it was he said to them. Only one or two peered into the car. The disassembling of the cross fascinated me until I realized the full significance: as each piece of pipe was removed, someone carried it off, I felt certain, to make pipe bombs.

"I'm sorry about lunch, Kate," Higgins said, scarcely aware, I was sure, he had said it. He had taken off his wristwatch, and watched time lessen the distance between O'Malley and Bakerstown.

"How many men does he have?" I asked.

"A hundred by now."

"And how much time do we have?"

"Ten minutes . . . I could go back to the club and call the governor, couldn't I? And maybe I'll have to. And maybe it's already too late."

I said, "I don't believe you will ever *have* to do anything, Steve." I think I meant it. I know I wanted to say the most reassuring thing I could.

Again he squeezed my hand. "We'll see. Now, just in case he comes, I would like you to sit on the other side of me. I want to be in the middle."

I had just changed places with him when Dingle said over his shoulder, "He's coming out, boss."

Down the walk George Canby came in great, long, loping strides. *Power to the people:* he gave the sign as he came, his fist in the air, and those along the way gave back the slogan.

Higgins edged forward and waited, his hand out. There was something in Canby's movement of both the dancer and the panther, that measured grace and speed which suggest perfect coordination. You never doubted either that he was aware of its effectiveness. His pause before the open car door was almost a "stop-camera." His one uncertainty was whether or not to take Higgins' hand.

I caught the slightest turn of that hand, a nuance of gesture that suggested Steve was about to withdraw it. Canby caught it: a brief grasp.

Steve said, "We ought to have done this sooner. Get in, young man, get in. You've met Mrs. Osborn. I understand you paid her a compliment in church this morning."

Canby maneuvered his head through the doorway as though he wore a bishop's mitre. Steve sat back. Canby perched almost on his haunches, one knee on the floor and one in the air. He balanced himself with a hand on the back cushion. He wore a necklace of bleached bone over a black tunic. What humanized him to me: the shabby, unpressed trousers and the worn shoes. He gave me a funny little nod as much as to say: You understand that was rhetoric this morning. Or so I chose to interpret him.

To Steve he said: "What's the man got to say to me that's important enough to take me away from my people?"

"There's no time left for bullshit, Canby. What do you think you'll accomplish with the fires and the bombs and the bricks? What good will it do them to burn themselves out of house and home?"

"That's one way of cleaning out the ghetto, boss."

"Fuck off, God-damn it. What do you want?"

Canby's teeth flashed. "You gave me the New Testament, boss. I'll give you the Old: an eye for an eye. Give us the killer and we'll take down the barricades."

"Do you want him dead or alive?"

"It don't matter."

"Do you want him from a tree or in the jail?"

"Oh, boss, you shouldn't ask that question trying to make peace with a black man."

"Strike it!" Higgins said.

Canby shrugged. "If you say so."

"I think we'll have the killer before the day is out."

"Who's *we?*"

"The people. Power to the people. Let's just say the people, Canby."

"As represented by the sheriff?"

"The sheriff, whether he likes it or not, will have the killer. Now I'm not going to lay it on the line any clearer than that."

"That's pretty clear—as far as it goes. Now what do you want from me?"

"I want you to turn around, shake your fist in the air so everybody out there can see it, and drive out of here with us right now."

"You're clear out of your head, man."

"Don't you know that O'Malley would rather have you right now than the killer?"

"Hell, yes. He doesn't want the killer."

"I mean he wants you badly," Steve said.

"Dead or alive?"

"It don't matter," Steve said, giving him back his own words. "It's a matter of minutes before he'll start to ring the ghetto with the Blue Hats—armed to the teeth, and with a bench warrant for your arrest."

"I'm waiting for him, boss. This time we're ready."

"He said the same Goddamned words, 'This time we're ready.' Canby, what if your people don't want to burn? What if they say to you, you don't live in Bakerstown? Remember last time?"

"I learned my lesson, boss. I'm a sleep-in lover of a well-known chick."

"But what if they say, George, go out and talk to the sheriff? What if they send you out to him when he bullhorns in his ultimatum?"

185

"They wouldn't do that to me."

"You'd burn them out to protect your skin."

"That's not the issue . . ."

"How many lives? How much blood?"

"On whose hands?"

"What the hell difference does it make? Dead is dead!"

Anderson was waiting a few feet away, talking, staying loose, but alert, on edge. Steve barked out his name. "Come over here!"

While Anderson came running I saw Dingle pick up a signal from Steve in the mirror.

"Shut that door," Steve commanded him.

And as Anderson slammed it shut, at the same instant Dingle rolled the car into motion, and since Canby was trying his best to open a door that would not budge for him, I realized Dingle controlled an inside lock from the dashboard.

"What the fuck's going on here?" Canby waved his hands wildly. "What are they standing out there doing nothing for? Stop the Goddamned car!" he shouted.

The people standing along the curb looked curious, surprised, but not especially alarmed. With the door closed, no one out there could see inside the car.

Steve pulled his neck in and thrust his fist in the air. "Power to Percy Anderson!"

Canby shouted at him, "Of all the stupid, motherfucking, Neanderthal . . ." He pounded his fists on the window and then tried to crack it with his elbow. The elbow would have broken easier, I thought possibly it did, for he writhed with the pain and rubbed and rubbed his arm, wrist to shoulder.

We passed through the police block without stopping.

"Look at them come, Steve," Dingle said over his shoulder.

We all looked toward the town where Dingle pointed. A procession of police cars was moving toward us, their red roof-lights circling. A fire truck followed, and another, and then more cars trailing out of sight.

"Take off, Dingie," Steve said. "Let's get out of their range before they see us."

Dingle turned us off Route 32, cutting over the curb and through a vacant lot, then rocking us back onto the pavement again. The three of us in the backseat looked out the rear window.

"Makes you feel important, doesn't it, Canby? A parade like that?"

Canby stuck his tongue in his cheek and then licked his lips. Bravura. Deep down he had to be relieved not to be facing that police juggernaut. But he said, "Man, I got to be important, if Steve Higgins is taking me for a ride."

Dingle turned into a dirt road that ran parallel to and presently rejoined the main road.

I said, "How long before O'Malley finds out what you've done, Steve?"

"A few hours. Long enough, I think. The regulars won't tell him. They're on our side."

"What *is* going to happen back there, boss?" Canby asked.

"I wish I knew. It depends on Anderson. And O'Malley. At least there won't be two hotheads toe to toe."

"Who are you to play God Almighty, man?"

"Someone with a little more experience at the game than you, that's all."

"Where are we going, Steve?" Dingle asked.

"Home. Why not? Laurie's holding court for us at the Mardi Gras. Our arrival in Venice was well advertised. Let's hole in behind the gates for a few hours and see what happens. How does that strike you, Canby? A weekend in the country."

"I should have brought my chick," he said, and threw an insolent glance at me. He was still sitting on the edge of the seat, his hand on the handle of the door.

Steve took the flask from his pocket, offered it first to me and, when I refused, to Canby.

Canby pretended not to see it. "Let the dead bury the dead: what kind of a message was that?"

"Why, I was saying that we revolutionaries ought to stick together: that's what I meant," Steve said.

"Ha!" Canby reached over and took the flask from his hand as Steve was about to take a drink himself.

Steve said, "I want to ask you something, Canby: in all seriousness, what's the difference between that . . . African halo you're wearing"—he described with a gesture of his hand the hairdo—"and a Blue Hat?"

Canby took a long drink of bourbon, shuddered with pleasure, and then answered. "To all practical purposes as far as you're concerned there isn't any difference. They just mean something to the people who wear them."

Steve nodded and took back the flask when Canby handed it to him. Both Canby and I watched him unhesitatingly raise it to his lips and drink after the black man. Canby's eyes and mine met. He broke the gaze instantly and ground his teeth as he looked out the window. Despite everything, he had cared that the man had not wiped the mouth of the flask before drinking, and he had been caught caring.

FIFTEEN

We sat very much with our own thoughts while Dingle pressed the accelerator almost to the floor. When we were near The Hermitage, Higgins said, "There's one thing I want you to understand, Canby: I don't approve of what you did to the sheriff this morning."

"I didn't ask for the ride, boss. You can put me down right now and I'll walk home. Tell you what else I'll do—I'll swear it was my idea that you get me out of there. I'll say I took my switchblade and put it to the little lady's throat . . ."

"Oh, shut up," Steve said. "All I'm saying is, sooner or later you're going to have to face those charges."

"I got that message, Mr. Higgins. And let me read the rest to you and see if it's as heavy as I think it is. That's going to be one sore-assed sheriff when he finds

190

out I'm gone, right? And not everybody in town drives a hearse like this, right? So if somebody spills, just how long do you figure it's going to take him to hounddog me, no matter where you hide me?"

"Cooling time. That's all I ask."

"Man, I think you should've let the fires burn. If he gets the opportunity, that pig is going to shoot me on the run. Then they'll really burn you out—the whole damn town. Only Georgie won't be around to enjoy it. Shit, brother, I just caught onto something. Out here he can shoot me at his convenience. And you can bury me where I'll be handy for digging up before, during, or after elections."

Steve said to me, "The boy has delusions of grandeur."

"I don't like you much, boss."

Steve chuckled.

After a moment Canby stretched his foot to toe the sheets where they lay on the floor. "What do they signify?"

"They're marked Good Samaritan Hospital," Steve said.

Canby shook his head. "The man sure has a fine sense of irony. Some good Samaritan that was." His realization was sudden: "Hey, the killer came that way, right? From the hospital?"

Steve brought out the card and showed it to Canby. "I don't suppose you recognize the writing?"

"That's printing."

I said, "Yeager thought it was you sent flowers to the hospital with that card."

"I dig . . . Somebody's trying to pin the Rhodes murder on me?"

"More delusions," Steve said, and replaced the card in the envelope and put it back in his pocket.

"Then what the fuck's it about? I never used the word "Niggertown" in my life. Niggerstown, that's different."

"With Gillespie's help we've figured all that out already," I said. "But it is about the killing of Parson Rhodes."

"The killing of Parson Rhodes," he repeated. "It sounds like a ballad. Maybe someday I'll write one . . ." He glanced at Steve and the spittle flew out with the words: "I know! More delusions! Go fuck yourself." He flung himself back in the corner.

Steve sat chuckling. "Did I say anything, Kate?"

Dingle all but put the Lincoln's nose through The Hermitage gate. He slammed on the brakes, hopped out, and limped rapidly into the gatehouse.

"This cat's even got his own penitentiary," Canby said, sitting up and looking out at the gate and the high fence.

When Dingle came with the key, a tall, gray-blond man was with him. I was a moment recognizing him.

"Who in hell is that?" Steve said.

"Randall Forbes."

"For Christ's sake, Kate. Didn't you get in touch with him?"

I was trying to open the car door, but it was locked.

"Get out and walk him up to the house," Steve said. "It will give us time."

"I can't get out!"

Canby sat back and howled at our frustration. It could not have been that funny. Or maybe it was. Not until Dingle returned and released the lock with the dashboard control was I able to leave the car. Forbes was standing by the open gate.

"Lock up and bring the key to the house, Kate," Higgins called out to me.

The car leaped past us before I reached Forbes' side.

Forbes said, "I hadn't expected to get here ahead of you, but I'm glad."

"Why, for heaven's sake?"

"Let it go that I'm glad," he said. "Do you know, they wouldn't let me in the house up there?"

"You weren't expected. I tried to reach you. I left a message at the physics department."

"The only message I got—I walked over to the Mardi Gras thinking I'd misunderstood you last night —and I was told you had just left in the limousine with Mr. Higgins."

"I'm sorry, Randall," I said. I closed the big gate with his help, locked it, and put the key in my pocket.

"Don't be sorry. Here I am on the inside. Or is that why you're sorry?"

We started up the graveled walk as the limousine disappeared from view. Forbes said, when I did not answer, "What a strange car that you can't see into. I'd have thought only movie stars and gangsters would ride in such."

I said, "A great many things have happened since I left your house last night." We seemed to be just off synchronization. I put it down to being tired and not having had anything to eat. "Why *did* you come? You must have known. I mean, you would know from the news that plans might have changed."

"I've told you, Katherine. I thought you were going to be here alone with him."

I glanced up at him. "And you were going to protect me?"

"Oh, go to hell," he said, the color flaming in his cheeks. "I came because I wanted to come, and I caught a ride from a milk truck that dropped me at the gate."

We walked in silence until the bend in the road.

"He does have a reputation, you know."

I said, 'Were you surprised to learn of Professor Lowenthal's Leipzig appointment?"

"I don't believe there was an appointment. The Communists are taking advantage of the tragedy to fabricate a propaganda situation. They may have approached him. There were opportunities. But I refuse to believe he would not have confided such intentions to me."

"Could that have been what he intended to tell you when he asked you to come to the office?"

"I have thought about that," he said.

"Do you know if there was a fan on in his office?" I asked without warning to either him or myself. To this day I have to say that I did not know I was going to ask such a question until it popped out.

"You are extraordinary!" he cried, his voice almost falsetto-high. "The police say the air conditioner had been turned on, the fan only."

And then I knew where the question had come from: when Forbes had turned on the fan in the jail, I thought it a most unlikely intelligence for him, such an expediency to block the effectiveness of a listening device. It would, however, occur to someone expecting bugs: like Lowenthal. One might suppose it was one more thing Forbes could have learned from the master. But when? That was the question.

We were approaching the house and I took for granted that there were servants about despite the closed-up look of everything. When we reached the terrace I could see Steve walking toward us within the house. I said, "What is it you want of me, Randall?"

"Redemption. Is that too big a word?"

*　*　*

Steve opened the door to us himself, having first to unlock and unbolt it. The whole staff seemed to have gone away. I did not look at Forbes although I was aware that he was watching my face for some sign; I think I was waiting for him to modify that "redemption," which hung over us, in those few seconds of waiting at the door, like a cardboard scimitar.

"I'm sorry I rushed ahead that way," Steve said, "but I had urgent business at the stable."

By which I assumed he was telling me that he had lodged Canby in the apartment there. He turned on more light in the hall, the better to see the tall man beside me. "So you're Forbes," he said. I had been waiting until he stood in one place to introduce them. "Well. You haven't chosen the best of times, but come along. Let's see what Cook has left for us to eat." He had not offered to shake hands, but now he took Forbes' arm and mine and steered us along with him.

"I cleared out everyone this morning. It promised to be one hell of a weekend, and so far it sure has come through on the promise, wouldn't you say, Kate?"

"That it has," I said.

"There was someone in here," Forbes said. "Someone who wouldn't answer the door."

"That'd be Paddy, the caretaker. He's not much for conversation."

We moved through the hall, hearing the phone ring. After two rings it stopped. Higgins explained that it was on an automatic answering device. The dining room seemed especially large and empty with its long and highly polished table. The landing field, sweeping beyond the windows there, looked the more desolate for the swirls of dust dervishing in the wind. The color of the light was eerie: the sun might yet come out before its setting.

Higgins brought a roast chicken from one of the refrigerators and hacked it into portions. With direction, I found bread and cheese and fresh butter in a crock. Steve chewed on a thigh while he put on water for coffee. Forbes sat on a stool, his arms folded, and watched. He looked as though he felt superior to the scene he was watching.

"Help yourself, for Christ's sake," Steve said, gesturing with the chicken thigh.

"Thanks," Forbes said with a little shake of the head. He did not otherwise move.

Steve set the bone down long enough to count the measures of coffee. He came back to the table and said, "Get yourself a chair, man. You're perched up there like a mother superior."

"Your hospitality is overwhelming," Forbes said,

and slowly descended from the stool. The color had risen as to two pinched spots in his cheeks.

"And so is your gall, sir." Steve took a last bite from the bone and then dropped it into a trash bucket alongside the table with a deliberateness that reminded me of his dropping the cup and saucer. I had had only a few bites of food, but I was no longer hungry.

Forbes did not sit down. He leaned against a counter as though bracing himself.

Higgins said: "How do you feel about your late boss going over to the Reds?"

"I don't believe it," Forbes said.

"Not even a little bit?"

Forbes did not answer, he knew he was being baited.

"Then how come you struck out the word, 'Leipzig,' from the obituary?"

"I didn't."

"Who did it then, the FBI?"

"I have no idea. Possibly the rewrite man, or whoever works on newspapers."

"It was done with an angry stroke, Professor. Fsst! fsst!" Higgins imitated the sound, and the stroke of a pen.

"Really."

"Like the dash of that hensfoot they call a peace symbol. On his desk. Remember?"

Forbes said nothing. His chin in his hand, he had one finger across his mouth. I felt that it gave him a sense of some self-control.

"I'm sure you know I own the newspaper," Higgins went on, almost amiably. "What you may not know is when I hire a man to edit, I expect him to edit and he knows it. My man caught that deletion and when the news came through he remembered. Now it's going to hurt the sheriff to have to question you, Professor. You're his kind of man, you know? . . . Or maybe it won't hurt him so much just now."

I saw the idea catching on with Higgins, the usefulness of Forbes as a prime suspect in the campus murder—to compensate O'Malley for his Bakerstown humiliation.

As abruptly as he had started his inquisition of Forbes, he dropped it. He turned to me. "Let's put off dessert till later, Kate. I want to find out what's going on back there if I can. Pick up the phone in a minute. I'm going to call from the office." On his way out he said to Forbes, "Relax, Professor. Have a drink. We may all have a cozy night together—a *ménage à trois,* isn't that what the French call it?"

I hardly knew how to face Forbes, alone. It was folly not to assume now that he was possibly a murderer, and yet I could not. The kettle had come to a boil. As I took the phone from its wall hook I said, "Why don't you make the coffee, Randall?"

He did not move for a moment. He said, "He calls you Kate."

"Yes," I said, snappish. "Most people do."

"Are you there, Kate?" Higgins said over the phone.

"I'm here."

"That'll keep the Professor's mind occupied for a while, won't it?" He was so damned cheerful. I listened to the dial signal.

After one ring: "Bakerstown Demo Club, Anderson speaking."

"What happened, Percy?"

"Steve, I just called you at the hotel . . ."

"I know. What happened?"

"It's okay so far . . ."

Even now I can see Forbes making coffee while I was listening to the phone conversation. Meticulously, he got a cloth from the sink and wiped up where the water had spilled, and then where Steve had spilled the ground coffee when he had measured it. My mind leapt at once to the wild mess in which Lowenthal's office had been left, presumably by his killer.

"Unless somebody gets gun-happy we'll come out all right," Anderson was saying.

"So much for the editorial. Give me the events. As they happened."

"Okay, Steve. When you were out of sight I went down to the first barricade and met O'Malley there. He started out by saying he would accept my proposition. I could get my own undertaker in there and he'd be willing to set up the autopsy right in the church. And, Steve? We're going to do that. I got Ida's consent to it just before coming back here."

"Good man," Steve said.

"I took credit myself for the compromise. It was easier than trying to explain."

"That's fine. That's why I'm called the boss and not the governor. Take it from where O'Malley agreed to the autopsy."

" 'Now,' he says, 'Send Canby out to me and we won't have any trouble.' I says, 'He's gone, Sheriff. You can come and look, but you won't find him.' Well, he threw that cold eye of his over all the barricades and black folk waiting, and he says, 'Tell me where he's gone to, and I'll tell you whether or not I believe you.' I said, 'What do you think I'm here for, John J? I'm here to cool things. I talked him into clearing out. He lives on campus. Try him there. And if you remember, John J.'—this is what I said to him—'if you remember, he walked out of Bakerstown after the riot last year when Parson Rhodes called him a Sunday patriot . . .' "

"Tell me tomorrow what *you* said, Percy. What did John Joseph say?"

"He called me a liar, that's what he said. But he marched back to where his men were waiting. And now he's got the place ringed off and I'm sure as hell glad Canby's out of here. If he was here we'd be blasting out and maybe blowing up the country."

"Get all that rhetoric out of your system, Percy, right now. You're Establishment, man. You're square like the rest of us, and thank God for it."

"Amen," Anderson said.

"How long before you think he'll move in?"

"After the autopsy. I figure every hour helps. It depends too, Steve. You know that's not exactly a Volkswagen you drove out of town in. And I'll tell you this: O'Malley and his specials gunned it out of here a lot faster than they came in."

"Percy," and I could hear the cold precision in Higgins' voice, "are you telling me that O'Malley is not in the vicinity of Bakerstown?"

"Not as of ten minutes ago when I came back

here. That's what I was trying to tell you in the first place."

I heard the click of the phone, and Anderson saying, "Steve?" I hung up the extension and set out cups and saucers. I was pouring coffee when Higgins reached the kitchen. He got out the cream and sugar for himself, saying nothing. After he had taken a couple of mouthfuls of coffee, he picked up the kitchen phone and dialed.

The phone rang several times at the other end. Higgins' frown deepened as he waited. Then I heard the woman's voice answer.

"Laurie? Where the hell were you? . . ." Sensing that something was wrong, he said, "Call me at home —three rings—hang up and dial again. Got it?"

"Steve . . ."

It was a man's voice and without answering, Higgins put the phone back on the hook. He looked at me. "That was O'Malley. I ought not to have made that call . . . God-damn Laurie!" He looked around as though for something on which to vent his anger. Almost literally his expression brightened as he seemed to rediscover Forbes' presence. "Well, Professor, how did you get out here? I didn't notice a car."

"I walked partway, and accepted a ride the rest."

"Ah, yes. You're a great walker, aren't you? Wouldn't you like a drink? Kate, play hostess for me. In the butler's pantry: find the makings."

I could not judge the motive in this false heartiness of his, if that's what it was. He was about to pick up the phone again, his hand resting on it. "We're still going to be waiting, all of us, but it may not be for as long as I thought. Get out the booze, Kate. Maybe we can all get to know one another before the roof falls in."

I said, "Will O'Malley . . ?"

He didn't let me finish. "I wouldn't be at all surprised."

He dialed an inside number. "Dingie? Did you put the limousine underneath? . . . Good. No lights. Even when it gets dark, and stay in there until you hear from me. Now send Paddy up to the house. Tell him to come round to the office. I'll let him in there." He looked at the phone before hanging it up. "Do you know what Dingie just said? 'Right on.'" Higgins grinned. "Remind me to tell you sometime how he lost his toes. Let me have the key to the gate."

I took it from my pocket and gave it to him. "Steve, why don't you just turn Canby loose?"

"Because he was right about his own position. By taking him out of the ghetto, I've set him up for a shot in the back. It's funny, but when you choose the lesser of two evils, you keep on having to make that same choice over and over again." He started out and then stopped to say to Forbes: "Do you know George Canby?"

Forbes said evenly: "Which of us is the lesser evil?"

"You're just too Goddamned clever, Professor. Bring the drinks upstairs. I'll see you in the library."

As soon as Higgins was gone Forbes said: "I want to talk to you, Katherine. He's an evil bastard."

I said, "I want you to go. Right now. Get off the estate any way you can, but go now."

"Not till I've talked with you."

"Then we'll walk," I said. I still had my coat on, for the kitchen was chilly. I motioned to Forbes to put his on. It lay on the stool where he had sat, as Higgins said, like a mother superior.

The wind came in gusts as we went away from the house. The sun rimmed the thick clouds with a white gold. It would set angrily within a few minutes. I wanted to get him as near the gate as I could.

"He thinks I killed Lowenthal," Forbes said, "and he wants to use me in some way. Don't you think?"

"Yes."

"And he's probably right."

"To use you?"

"About Lowenthal, I mean."

We both lowered our heads into the wind. I said, my face toward him, " 'Probably' is not an admissible word under the circumstances, Randall."

Silence except for the scraping of gravel under our feet.

"You know that there was no foundation grant," he said at last.

"You made it up?" I said slowly.

"To impress you, that's all I had in mind at first. And I wanted to know how it would feel—how it would have felt. I'd been crushed in Chicago. The old man had prophesied that. So I began to make it up on the train . . . For God's sake, let's stand still and talk. We may never have another chance."

"All right," I said. "Let's get off the road, the woods may shelter us a little."

A few yards brought us through to the bridle path where I had first seen Higgins and Laurie. The wind was quieter there.

"I made it up the way it should have gone—I'd made the presentation weeks before, you see. I'd merely gone up because I'd asked them for a verbal answer. Somehow I'd thought . . ." He shrugged. "It doesn't matter."

"I was impressed," I said, and started us walking again, but more slowly.

"And you believed me and then I thought you might tell Higgins. And it had felt so good to celebrate, you know. So I told Lowenthal, and he believed me, and he told Bourke and I came almost to believe it myself."

"Oh, Randall," I said. "I'm so sorry."

"Don't be. I'm not telling you this part to make you feel guilty. In fact, I'm thanking you in a way. It showed me something that I wouldn't otherwise have ever learned: The fault, dear Brutus, you know? He's got me doing even that like him. I'd always felt the fault lay in my stars, and it didn't. I could have made it on my own. Oh, Katherine, what if I confess and they don't believe me?"

"Then you will have to believe them," I said, although I thought: they will believe you.

"I am mad, I suppose. I don't feel mad. It is no accident, the misuses of that word for anger. But you know, I think it works the other way: it is the lack of anger that makes one mad . . ."

I heard a sound on the gravel and put my hand out to silence Forbes. A man wearing a cap, his head bent to buck the wind, was riding a bicycle toward the gate. I supposed it was Paddy.

When he was out of hearing, I said: "Lowenthal did tell you that he was going to Leipzig, didn't he?"

204

"That's what he brought me to the office for, to tell me that. He was afraid that the FBI had tapped his house in some way. And in the office, he turned on the fan before we talked. He had said to me what I said in the jail, 'X cancels Y.' But he wouldn't believe me about there being no foundation grant. That's the craziest part of the whole story. He simply would not believe me. It suited him not to. He had, in those few hours, built his escape from me on *my* fantasy: Randall, the achiever, the self-reliant. I kept saying it was a joke, a fantasy I had tried out on a woman, and that he should have known. Then he said if that were so, I had done it deliberately to make a disgrace of myself, which he would not believe. 'You have too much dignity for that, Randall. Too much pride.' Dignity and pride, and me with the tears in my eyes, begging him to find a place for me in Leipzig. I seem to remember him saying, 'Peace, Randall,' and starting for the door. I remember the wall clock saying ten-thirty with its second hand frozen at two. I don't know why I remember that but I do, and after that nothing . . ."

I visualized the clock: questioning whether its face resembled the peace symbol. Not exactly, but neither was the mind perceiving it exact.

"Nothing, nothing until I was sitting in the bar at the Mardi Gras wishing I could get at you. That's what I felt, but gradually it changed and I felt a kind of forgiveness toward you—and what I said a few minutes ago came through to me, that I was perfectly capable on my own. Which is what I meant when I used that word, 'redemption.' I do love melodrama, don't I? But Katherine, I swear to you, I walked home that night saying to myself, I'm going to leave the old man. He's got a son. I'm going to run away from home. And then, when they got me out of bed in the morning, I was shocked—and hurt—and then the anxiety began to close in . . . I did try to get them to take my clothes. If I did it, there has to be blood . . ."

We were near the gate house and I stopped. "How did you get on the grounds? Wasn't the gate locked?"

"Through the gate house. Both doors were unlocked."

"What I shall do, Randall, is make a commotion at the gate. It's almost dark in the shadows round the house. You ought to be able to slip out the way you came in." I realized I was holding his hand.

"I oughtn't to leave you here alone with him."

"It won't be for long," I said. "There's going to be trouble here, and you have enough of your own."

"Are you afraid of me?"

"No."

He squeezed my hand and let it go. "But you would be . . . Good-bye . . ."

I left him without saying anything more. I took off my wristwatch and put it in my pocket. Then I stuck my head in the door where the sullen-looking Irishman was sitting with his pipe. "I lost my watch, Paddy, when I locked the gate this afternoon . . ."

The decoy worked.

SIXTEEN

Higgins was watching for me at the library window. I saw him leave the window as I approached, so I went to the front door, which he opened to me. We did not speak until we got into the library.

"Did you think I'd have him lynched?"

"He wasn't supposed to be here," I said. "It seemed better that he go."

"He couldn't have gone any faster on wings. Do you think he's guilty, Kate?"

"I don't know."

"That's a positive answer." He got out the whiskey decanter and glasses.

I took off my coat and warmed my hands at the fire. It had only begun to catch. I could hear the pipes throughout the house where the heat was starting to come up.

Higgins brought two glasses, an inch and a half of

bourbon in each. He gave me one of them, and studied the glass in his hand for a moment. "I like my whiskey straight, my men he . . . Cheers." He held the liquid in the back of his throat for a second or two, his head back, his eyes closed, and then swallowed. When he opened his eyes he was looking at the portrait of Jackson. "What would you do in my position, Mr. President?"

Old Hickory. I too half-listened in the silence for an answer.

"You know, Kate: it's not the hide of a man, it's the principle of the matter."

I thought about that, taking a mouthful of bourbon. "I think he'd have disagreed with you on that, Steve. I don't think Jackson ever felt as passionate about a principle as he did about people. And when they were wrong, he was even more passionately concerned about them."

After a moment he said: "I could go to school to you, Kate."

"God forbid! What an end to a beautiful friendship."

He grinned and pointed a finger at me. "Mind, there's a thing or two in which I might be able to instruct you on the way." He returned to the window. It was almost entirely dark. "Damn this waiting," he said.

"The barbarians are coming today."

"What?"

"It's a poem," I said. "*From* a poem."

"Say it for me."

"I can't. But they were waiting, and then the barbarians never came. It was a disappointment. The last line goes, 'Those people were a kind of solution.'"

He grunted: it was not his style. "I've turned off the phones up here," he said, "to stay clear for Paddy."

And before I quite understood it, the bell rang—more a buzz than a ringing—a separate line.

He crossed the room in long, quick strides. "Yes, Paddy?" I heard the Irishman's voice, for he shouted in the manner of one not accustomed to the telphone. Higgins was slow to answer. Then: "Send her up and then lock the gate again."

"Laurie?" I said.

He shook his head. "Annie . . . the sheriff's wife."

I said, "I think I'll go down to the kitchen and get something to eat after all," and picked up my coat.

He watched me almost to the door. "What kind of a newspaper woman are you, Kate, to walk out on the appearance of a principal witness?"

I went back and sat down in my old chair before the fire, and waited.

❊   ❊   ❊

"She stays, Annie. She was invited. You weren't."

She looked deathly tired, blue under the eyes, and her blond hair wild. "You're going to tell him, aren't you, Steve? To save the black man."

"We lost a black man this morning, Annie, remember? Sit down."

She continued to stand, her hands working deep in her pockets. "It wasn't supposed to happen . . . Get her out of here, Steve. Please. I want to talk to you. You owe it to me."

"She stays, Annie."

"I don't trust her."

I said, "You can always sue for libel, Mrs. O'Malley."

Higgins looked at me. "Would you say the same to me, Kate? Am I to get that message too? Because if I am, you've missed the whole point to Steve Higgins. There isn't anything Annie can tell you about her and me I wouldn't tell you about myself. There isn't anything anybody can tell you that I'd deny. There's things been said about me that would grow hair on a corpse, and the day I start denying them, Kate, is the day the people are going to start believing them."

"Please, Steve, before John Joseph comes . . . I don't want to do him harm . . ."

"Why doesn't he come if he's coming?" Higgins said.

"Soon . . . too soon," she said in a kind of whimper.

I went to the window and watched. It was better than watching either of them, and I thought of the things about Higgins I had learned within the last hour.

She went close to Higgins and whispered to him. I saw the movement out of the corner of my eye.

Higgins repeated aloud what she had said: " 'Tarkie says nobody needs to know I was there . . .' "

"God-damn your soul, Steve Higgins. I hope you roast in hell."

Higgins laughed. "That's more like the Annie I used to know."

I experienced what I thought was *déjà vu*, but it wasn't, and I remembered the association: Gilly saying to the obscenity-spouting Yeager: that's more like my

boy. Meanwhile I had been watching, without aware-
ness of what I was watching, tiny pinpricks of light in
the distance—like firebugs intermittently luminous.
Firebugs in March?

"Steve, I think there are men with flashlights coming up through the woods."

He reached for the phone and dialed. There was
no answer. He strode out of the room then and I
grabbed my coat and followed him. He opened the
vestibule door and we stepped out on the terrace. The
air was damp and raw with the promise of snow in it.
"Where did you see them?"

I pointed to the right. "They'd be headed toward
the barns, I think. Otherwise wouldn't they come up
the drive?"

"That informing son of a bitch," he said of Paddy.

We listened for a minute. The only sound was the
muffled lowing of cattle. "It's milking time," he said.
"There'll be dairymen in the barn, but the groom's
gone home by now." He stepped back into the house,
got a sheep-lined coat from the closet, and then
opened a switch box. "We'll be lit up like Venice," he
said, pulling one switch after another.

The terrace when we stepped out on it was in
brighter light than that day's daylight had been. I ran
to keep up with him. The yard, around which was the
complex of farm buildings, stable, cowbarn, dairy,
corncribs, was also flooded with light. But not a soul
was to be seen. Lights burned in the cowbarn, but the
stable was in darkness: one had to look closely to be
sure with so much light outside.

In the center of the yard Steve stopped. He

cupped his hands around his mouth and shouted: "Do you have a search warrant, Sheriff? If you have, we'll do business."

O'Malley and his specials came out of the shadows, eight or nine men wearing blue hats, most of whom I recognized. Tarkington was among them. So was Paddy. O'Malley showed the warrant. "I want the black boy, Steve."

Higgins gave the warrant but a glance. "Didn't Paddy tell you, a half-hour ago . . . after I got you instead of Laurie . . . ?"

"It's no good, Steve. I want him." He put the warrant back in his pocket.

"What about the murderer of Rhodes?"

"First things first. You know I'll burn that barn down to get him, Steve."

"One horse harmed, O'Malley, and I will cut your throat myself."

O'Malley smiled; a cold smile, but one that somehow sent a thrill of excitement through me. He could taste success. "Steve . . ." and now he spoke with a marvelous relaxation, "you know there isn't a nigger alive worth coming between two white men. Not after what we've been through together."

Steve wasted very little time, that was to be said for him, he moved quickly. He cupped his hands again and shouted toward the stable: "Dingie? Bring him out! Dingie? Turn on the upstairs light if you hear me."

And a second or two later, the light went on.

I was standing near Steve Higgins and the sheriff. O'Malley said, but softly and intended for Higgins only, I think: "I know who killed the parson. It's just too damn bad it had to happen to one of my men."

Higgins said, "But isn't he here, John Joseph?"

"Like I said, first things first."

I looked at Tarkington. He was standing as tense as a steeple, his shotgun ready, and I knew why O'Malley had ordered his priorities.

The stable door opened slowly. It was Dingle who came out first, his hands in the air, and with Canby as close behind him as his shadow. Dingle tried to speak, but he couldn't, a wavering croak.

Steve shouted: "Let them go! For Christ's sake, let them go! He's got Dingie's gun in his back."

"You better believe him, man, because if we don't drive out of here as safe as we drove in, here's one dead cat. You believe me, don't you, little fellow?"

"Steve." Dingle's voice cracked on the word.

"Canby, let him go," Higgins said. "I give you my word."

"Your word, boss? How many times?" He jabbed Dingle in the back with the gun. "Come on, little man. Let's get to that fucking machine and get me out of here."

With the first steps they took, all the deputies took aim.

"For Christ Jesus' sake, O'Malley. Call them off!" Higgins pleaded.

"Hold your fire." O'Malley glanced at Tarkington, his expression: nobody wins.

I walked across the yard between the men and Canby and Dingle. "I'm coming too," I called out.

There was no sound from anyone for a moment.

The black man and his hostage moved from sight around the corner of the stable. After I had passed that way too, I heard the jeers and catcalls from the sheriff's men.

I helped Dingle open a wagon door at the far end of the stable. Nothing showed but a great stack of hay. Both Canby and I realized that the hay had been released from the loft on top of the limousine.

"Burrow in, little man, and bring it out." Then, half to me: "Would there be a gun in that car?"

"I don't think so, but I'll go in with him."

"Nigger lover," Canby said and showed his teeth. He decided against even that much trust. The three of us flailed our way through the loose hay and got into the car. We went out from the barn blind, but once outside the hay disappeared in the wind.

It was I who opened the gate, following Dingle's instructions on where to get a second key in the lodge. Three cars from the sheriff's office were parked outside the gate. I watched for Forbes on the road, and within a few miles, we passed him. I asked Dingle to stop, but we drove on, obeying Canby's orders.

Canby, much to my surprise, got out of the limousine at the Bakerstown barricade and surrendered himself to the regulars and the black municipals on duty there. He gave Dingle back his gun.

Poor Dingle. He said to me, "Can you drive, missus? My legs is all water."

I agreed to drive him and the car as far as the Mardi Gras.

Canby looked at me as I got out of the back and into the driver's seat. My own legs had felt stronger, and to drive that brute any distance, I would have needed them to be much longer. Canby grinned at me. "You know what you're driving, don't you, sweetheart? The God-damnedest biggest phallus in the world."

SEVENTEEN

I stayed on for a few days with Norah and Gilly.

A telegram on the night of my return from The Hermitage terminated Higgins' consent to a *Saturday* profile. No explanation. Like dropping a cup and saucer.

Mike, when I called him, said to cover the news angle and come home.

Home.

Tarkington was arrested by the sheriff at noon on Sunday, charged with the first-degree murder of Stanley Rhodes. After which O'Malley resigned. There is no doubt whatsoever in my mind that he will soon be back in office.

It may well be that when we passed Forbes on the road that night, I became the last person who recognized him to have seen him alive. It was late that night or early morning that he drowned himself in the campus lagoon, jumping from the bridge beneath which the ice was thin. His body was not found until midweek. By which time a nationwide alarm was out for him in connection with the murder of Daniel Lowenthal.

However, other trouble was plaguing Venice by then; the coal miners walked out Monday morning. Ostensibly the strike owed to the unsafe dust conditions in the Red Devil Mines, but it coincided with the announcement in the *Downstate Independent* of the revised hiring policy whereby any veteran, black or white seeking work in the mines . . .